THE LOVE OF SINGULAR MEN

THE LOVE OF
SINGULAR MEN

Victor Heringer

translated from the Portuguese by James Young

A NEW DIRECTIONS
PAPERBOOK ORIGINAL

Originally published in Brazil by Companhia das Letras
as *O amor dos homens avulsos*

Published in agreement with Redondo Books International Literary
Agency and Peirene Press. With special thanks to Sophie Lewis, who provided
editorial support as part of the Peirene Stevns Translation Prize mentorship
established with the generous support of Martha Stevns. James Young
would like to thank Alice Sant'Anna and Eduardo Heringer for their help
with queries on the original text, and Professor Omoniyi Afolabi
for providing information on the Yoruba language.

First published by New Directions in 2023 as NDP1573
ISBN 978-0-8112-3747-5
Manufactured in the United States of America
Design by Erik Rieselbach

Library of Congress Control Number: 2023016480

4 6 8 10 9 7 5 3

New Directions Books are published for James Laughlin
by New Directions Publishing Corporation
80 Eighth Avenue, New York 10011

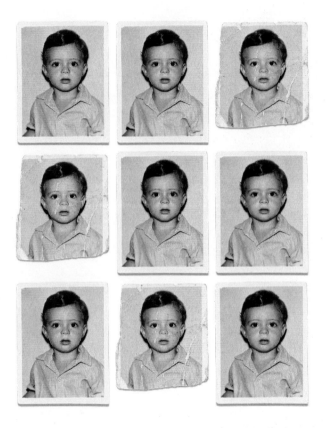

As soon as born the infant cries,
    For well his spirit knows,
A little while, and then he dies,
A little while, and down he lies.

—Christopher "Kit" Smart, the lunatic
Hymns for the Amusement of Children (1771)

A thousand unborn eyes weep with his misery.
Antinous is dead, is dead forever.

—Fernando Pessoa

WEATHER REPORT
The temperature of this novel is always over 88°F.
Relative humidity: never below 59%.
Wind speed: never exceeds 4 mph in any direction.

The sea is a long way from this book.

1

In the beginning, our planet was hot, sickly yellow and stank of stale beer. The ground was black with boiling, clinging mud.

The outer suburbs of Rio de Janeiro were the first things to come into this world, even before the volcanoes and the sperm whales, before Portugal invaded, before President Getúlio Vargas ordered the construction of social housing. Queím, where I was born and grew up, is one of those suburbs. Tucked between Engenho Novo and Andaraí, it was made from that primordial sludge, which coagulated into various shapes: stray dogs, flies and steep hills, a train station, almond trees and shacks and houses, neighborhood bars and arsenals of war, haberdasheries and *jogo do bicho* lottery stands and an enormous swathe of land reserved for the cemetery. But it was all still empty: there were no people.

They didn't take long. The streets collected so much dust that man had no choice but to come into being to sweep them. And in the late afternoons, to sit on the porch and moan about poverty, bad-mouth others and gaze out at the pavements stained by the sun, the buses coming back from work coating the world with dirt again.

2

I read in one of my schoolbooks that, near the hottest parts of the earth, there existed a race of people that despised the sun. ⁙ The men hurled insults in its direction five times a day and prayed joyfully when night fell. At the first glimpse of its rays, the women covered their heads and eyes with plain muslin, just as they did when they buried their dead, and only uncovered themselves at dusk. Because of the sun, these people were black and their continent was called Africa.

Though I'm so white I'm almost green, I am a child of this people. I've hated the sun since I was a kid, but all my life it's been licking me like a puppy. I've learned to tolerate its presence, occasionally even believed I loved it, but it's no good: I hate the sun. I mutter obscenities at it five times a day.

In the school holidays of 1976, I was thirteen. The summer hadn't even really begun and my skin was already peeling for the third time. My arms and shoulders, inflamed with tiny blisters, soon shed strips of dead tissue. My nose had a new layer of charred skin. I couldn't brush my hair because of my toasted scalp, nor sleep because of my back. It was almost noon already.

We'd been in the pool since morning. Joana, my younger sister, dived, floated and giggled, wearing only her bikini bottoms, despite her already swollen nipples. I couldn't swim, so I had to sit on the edge of the pool, with my feet in the water and my thighs on the hot granite, watching the sun slowly nibble away at the patches of shade. Sitting on the second-floor balcony, Maria Aína kept an eye on us while Paulina, the maid, took care of lunch, and the dust.

By my childish calculations, Maria Aína must have been around 279 years old. She lived in the neighborhood and looked after us whenever Mama asked. (I don't know if she got paid.) She was born right here in Queím, died here and lived here, in a shack that had been around since the days when the neighborhood was a farm. She'd never been outside Rio—the furthest she'd ever traveled was Jurema, where the spirits of the Indians dwell.

She gave long whistles as she breathed, like an old animal, and had witnessed the birth of every living person, including my dad. Thin, the daughter of slaves, she spoke the tongue of her great-great-grandparents when she didn't want to be understood. When she looked at green fruit it would ripen. She'd make pumpkin compote on the Day of Saints Cosmas and Damian, and bring it to us still warm. I've never forgotten the taste, or how the crunchy shell would break to reveal the gritty, pulpy cream. We were the first to eat it, after the spirits: she'd leave a bowlful in the woods for them. The pumpkin would shrivel up and vanish. That's how spirits eat.

Maria Aína liked me because I'd been born with the umbilical cord wrapped around my neck, just like her. "Anyone born that way will always be on the edge of trouble, *ossí* Camilo," she told me, years later, only days before she died.

3

Joana swam to the edge and splashed water on my legs to soothe my burns. She got out of the pool and protected me with a parasol. I still remember the face she made when she looked after me: a shy smile, tight-lipped on account of her missing teeth, her eyebrows sad and solemn, because I couldn't walk as well as her. I had a weak leg. Monoparesis of the lower left limb. I was crippled, but not terribly. By five, I was limping; by eight, I was on crutches.

In the school holidays, I hid my crutches and used a staff made from the wood of a guava tree, almost as tall as I was, and curved at the end. I felt wild when I used it, a wanderer or a shaman, a boy like any other. (Most of the time I had to hold myself up with both hands.) Today, that same piece of wood serves me as a cane. It's supported me as I've grown old. It used to belong to a relative of Maria Aína, and she gave it to me. I don't know who made it, but it's one of the things I love the most. When I'm in a sentimental mood, I can feel the soul in everything made from that same wood.

I've never been able to stomach guavas.

Joana dived back into the water. After swimming aimlessly for a few minutes, she came over again. She grinned, displaying the gaps in her teeth.

I knew that grin. She wanted to tell me something. My sister was mortified by those gaps, but grinned whenever she wanted to reveal or discover secrets. To show that her mouth held no mysteries, that her tongue would do no harm. She was an open child. (When Mama died, at the beginning of this century, Joana smiled broadly, then broke the news.)

"Mama didn't water the plants, she didn't water them again today," she said, making a face like a sleuth. To prove it, she jumped out of the pool, skipped over to the flower beds and came back with a few fern leaves. I pinched one, and it crumbled between my fingers. The sun had scorched Mama's garden. She couldn't have watered it in weeks.

Joana asked me something with her eyebrows. I flapped my lips in a gossipy, fishlike manner. She exhaled, imitating the adults, hands on hips, rolling her eyes. She knew a lot more than me, but even so, she knew nothing at all.

I had only one fear: if the plants dried out, they'd soon turn yellow. If they turned yellow, autumn would come early, and summer would be over. With no summer, there'd be no summer holidays. We'd have to go back to school.

We had no idea of the problems that had plagued our parents' marriage in recent months. We didn't even know who ran the country. We lived under the weird dictatorship of childhood: we looked but didn't see, listened but understood nothing, spoke and were largely ignored. But we were happy under that regime. Like a thick shroud, the fabric of our young lives shielded us completely.

The first rip appeared that day. The sound of our father's car reached our ears. Light invaded our hiding place. Vrum-vru-rum, there was his Corcel turning the corner. It stopped in front of the gate and growled again—vroo-vroom—demanding to be let in. No one went to open the gate. Mama appeared on the balcony, exchanged a few words with Maria Aína, made as if to stay, then went back inside. Dad, who was lifting up the iron gate, didn't see her. He parked in front of the pool, honked his horn, and the sun struck the mucus-yellow bodywork of the Corcel and blazed right into our eyes.

4

Maria Aína got up slowly, her skeletal frame weary and stiff, and stood gazing down on us. Joana brought my staff and helped me up, her gap-toothed smile demanding to know what gifts Dad had brought us, because he always brought presents back from his trips. He got out of the car, slammed the door and exhaled heavily as he adjusted his pants. This heat. Engine off, the Corcel purr-purred asthmatically, then finally went to sleep. My sister gave a squeal and hurriedly wrapped herself in a towel.

It was only then I saw his head framed by the rear window. The shaved head of a boy as much a boy as me.

But I had a full head of hair and I wasn't that coffee-with-watered-down-milk color. I was red in the summer, and greenish white in winter. His skull must always have been that same mixture of colors. He looked strong; I was skinny, more breakable, lame. But his eyes looked fragile, like the neck of a small bird, or a puppy that finds itself caught in a rattrap.

My first instinct was to hate him. I wanted to poke out his eyeballs, make him disappear from the face of the earth. Who knows why. Hate has neither reason nor purpose. Love has purpose, but not hate. Love perpetuates the human race, protects us from sterility and the deadliest solitudes. Hate is bigger, has more tentacles, and speaks with more mouths than love. Love is a physiological function; hate is a sublime and furious hunger. It's the reason we're the dominant species on the planet. Hate is the perpetration of the species.

I hated Dad's voice saying "Come on, come on out," and I hated how slowly the boy slunk through the half-open door of the car, and I hated his name—"This is Cosme," Dad said—and I hated the baby-blue shirt he was wearing (bought by Dad, I was sure), and his awkward run into the wings of *my* father, who wrapped him in that big embrace of his. I hated with an ancient hate, in a language only Maria Aína could understand and which I would never decipher.

Wrapped in a towel up to her almost-breasts, my sister strode snootily up to the boy, looked him right in the eye, and gave him a suspicious hello. He helloed her back, his chin glued to his chest, and I hated his scaredy-cat voice. She told him her name was Joana and held out her hand. He took it, bowing like a proper gentleman. Dad hawhawed at the mini adults and looked over at me, tears of laughter still in his eyes. I realized I was only wearing my swimming trunks, vulnerable and almost naked—propped up on a guavawood crutch like a horrendous lemur.

I must have felt embarrassed, because I imagined I heard Mama's voice. From inside the house, calling my name. Her everyday call, as though she wanted me to try on new pajamas, or drink some cherry cough syrup, which I loved and would drink without complaint. Although imaginary, her call was an irresistible magnet, far more powerful than the fear I felt at my dad's voice, though that was big, bigger than a city block. I had to go. I excused myself, without looking back at this new Cosme, and hobbled off in the direction of the house. Dad didn't try to stop me. A boy child belongs to his mother.

"Tell her we're here."

I turned and made a shield with my hand, to protect my eyes from the loathsome sun. Then I asked if this was our new little brother. I did this to hurt them. Every face turned toward my dad's.

He started to explain, but ended up explaining nothing: "Yes, well, no …" Cosme hung on his words. His mouth opened a crack, as though he were seeing a jewel beetle for the first time.

5

Number 47, Rua Enone Queirós, formerly Avenida Suaçu. The address of my childhood home. Three floors, four bedrooms, one en suite, six bathrooms. A living room and a dining room, balconies, the maids' room. A big garden, with a swimming pool. An avocado tree, a palm tree (the palm was mine, the avocado was Joana's), a variety of shrubs, an electric fence, undesirable creatures, hosts of insects, every now and then an opossum. A family neighborhood, a good distance from the favelas. Thriving shops and businesses, a bus stop outside the gate.

These days, it's two blocks from one of the biggest shopping malls in the North Zone of Rio, and about four blocks from the apartment where I live now (two bed, one en suite). After more than thirty years away, I came back to Queím. I want to die right where I was born. Everyone likes a little symmetry.

They knocked down pretty much the entire neighborhood. All that's left on Rua Enone is the facade of the old slave house, which dates back to the days of the Queím farm and is protected by the heritage department. And it really is just the facade: they turned the rest into a parking lot. Here and there plate glass buildings have sprung up in place of the dilapidated town houses. The streets have been paved and the street corners brightened up by the electric company. Everything's shrunk.

This city suffers from a fever which, every once in a while, causes these belle epoque hallucinations. *Knock it down, let's start all over again!* It's the modernizing parasite, the Miami malaria, which before that was the Paris malaria. During the last bout of delirium, they ripped out a scenic mountain to bury a sliver of sea, and sanitized everything. Next, I'm sure, they'll sanitize the locals, once and for all.

Anyway.

Today the house where I grew up belongs to the owner of a well-known building-supplies store. It's soared in value. If Joana and I hadn't sold it when Mama died, I'd be a lot better off now. But what's done is done; the owners of the farm that gave the neighborhood its name must have thought the same thing: ah, if only we hadn't sliced the place into lots and sold it all to those wretched little people!

6

Mama spent the rest of the day locked in her room. The official orders were to leave her in peace, she needed rest: headache, dizziness, effects of the heat. While she was in there, Dad fixed up the maids' room (Paulina never spent the night) for Cosme: a mattress, sheets, water, "What else?" clothes he wore when he was a boy (which would never have fit me), Mickey Mouse comics. The boy followed him around, his mouth hanging open, saying yes to everything, both of them trailed by Joana, helpful and a little overexcited. I spied on them from afar, sitting on the rocking chair in the living room, my staff planted on the floor for leverage. I tried to make my eyebrows thick and glowering, because that's how I imagined people showed anger.

Darkness fell quickly. Soon after the boy went into his room and shut the door for the night, everyone else did the same. Paulina went home early, Maria Aína made herself scarce. The dogs in the street ceased their howling. There wasn't a breath of air.

The small, sweltering hours of the night stole in through the gaps in the windows and doors. The silence of the crickets ruled, willing to abdicate only when the sun reassumed power, but Mama and Dad's voices staged a coup. The walls, mouths closed, chewed up their words, but I knew the sound was anger and that they weren't laughing at anything funny. They were fighting.

Sometimes there were long periods of peace until the cease-fire ended and the hum of hate grew again. I was desperate to creep closer, to hear better, but my shuffling and the tap-tap of my staff would have given me away. I stayed in my room. Suffocated mutterings. Suddenly, a clearly audible note: a door slam! Another: a cry fired into the air, before falling unanswered into the silence. The crickets.

In the middle of this muted din, Cosme escaped. He opened a door, jumped out of a window, whatever—the house slept unlocked. And with no idea where to go, he ran, muscles as wiry as a street cat's. Lamppost bumps, curbstone trips, sweat. After half an hour, the streets blurred into one and he came across a big, elongated building, with no doors and holes where the windows should have been. And inside there was nothing, just a roofless waste ground.

The sky began to turn lilac.

The sun took us by surprise. Dad got up early to take the boy a glass of milk and only managed to find him an hour later.

Cosme had hidden in the old slave house, which even back then was only a facade. The black residents of the neighborhood, many of whom were related to the slaves who'd worked on the farm, were understandably fearful of the building. They'd only go there with Maria Aína, to speak and dance with the black saints. The Catholics among them wouldn't even do that. Today, the front of the building remains, but the land behind has been turned into a parking lot, and everyone is evangelical. If the saints are still there, their lungs must be ruined.

Stupid boy, Cosme, ass. I can almost see him: nearly four feet tall, ninety pounds of brown flesh sweating and shivering in the abandoned slave house, sure they'd never find him. Instinctively, it was the first place Dad went to look for him.

7

Cosme didn't try to run away again. He spent the next few days sulking, sitting in his room, whimpering. He only came out when he was called twice, three times, five times. He didn't speak. When we gave him food, he kept his distance, dragged the plates across the floor of his room, ate with his hands and spat, the age-old sulk of punished kids. On the days when Mama wasn't home, he'd sit at the table with us (Dad gave him little choice), but refuse to eat.

Mama took a lot of trips during those school holidays. It was the year my maternal grandmother died, alone and inconvenient. She lived near Campos. Mama had plenty of grudges against her, and no sisters; she had to take care of her illness and the funeral, which were both at least brief. Dad worked long hours as a doctor and frequently got called in urgently. So we were often left alone with Paulina. Sometimes Maria Aína appeared to help with lunch or keep an eye on the children.

I wasn't allowed to play in the street. A crippled boy wouldn't last long among the kids of Queím. Joana wasn't allowed out because she was a girl. We read, we drew, TV wasn't as good as it is today.

Back then I wasn't the old hyena I am now. I had the whole world to experience before it ended. I liked Jules Verne, H. Rider Haggard, journeys around the world and *Treasure Island*. I dreamed about the road to Minas Gerais (were there gold mines? Were there still slaves, talking oxen, tree spirits, kings named Solomon?) and planned to become God and create a planet. How did the smell of coffee get invented? The colors of our skins? Other civilizations?

I had a certain love of men.

Today it seems foolish.

8

I've never seen anything that filled me with more dread than Maria Aína cooking ox tongue. One day, just before lunchtime, a warm-sour smell drew me to the kitchen. There was the old woman, sweating through her mustache (a few thick, white hairs on her upper lip). The pressure pot steaming, psst-psst, psst-psst. She was teaching Paulina that to cook the meat you first had to peel the skin from the tongue. You had to boil it and slice it off at the roots, but even then it wouldn't come off easily. "You have to pull really hard," she said, her gnarled fingers digging, scraps of skin stuck to the backs of her damp hands.

I imagined her fingers pulling a shred of burnt skin from my shoulder, the shred becoming a strip and soon a long ribbon running down my back, a thousand specks of blood blossoming. I imagined Paulina laughing darkly. I shivered so violently I almost slipped and fell.

Maria Aína looked at me and smiled. She must have spotted the disgust on my face because she said: "Do you want to take a look, *ossí* Camilo? Do you know what that smell is? It's the smell of all the words the ox can't say." Paulina laughed. (Her fingernails were really long, the color of red wine, like the shell of a cockroach.) She was already pregnant but can't have known it.

That was the day it happened. When lunch was on the table, Paulina called us and Cosme came out of his room, freshly showered, white shirt buttoned up to his Adam's apple. He sat with us, very politely, and ate the tongue with potatoes that Maria Aína had prepared, and the old woman smiled and murmured approvingly: "*dejú* Cosme, *dejú* …" And he answered— and asked what we were eating, and what team we supported, and if there were fries, and if this, and if that, and pleases and thank yous.

I didn't enjoy my lunch. I didn't go near the meat. Dread in the pit of my stomach. I was sure the boiled tongue of the ox had something to do with the loosening of the boy's tongue.

9

I still remember the smell of Maria Aína, the perfume of the brownish cream she put in her hair. Paulina too. I remember the leathery black skin of their feet (it looked so much thicker than mine). The tenderness I sometimes feel toward them both, if it swells a little more, turns to pain. As far as I know, they're buried right here in Queím. Ambition has probably scattered their children all over the country. I'll never discover where they ended up; no one knows the humble fates of so many people. They probably became gardeners, *jogo do bicho* lottery-ticket sellers, barroom drunks, maybe, if they were lucky, industrial automation technicians.

The neighborhood cemetery lies in a ravine which used to fill with mist on cold mornings. These days there are no cold mornings in the suburbs. They say the planet will end in sweat and floods. If that's true, the world began to end in Queím, and not recently either. Every summer here there are floods, shacks tumbling down hills, water shortages and power cuts. My father said when he was a child the water froze in the taps on winter mornings. And you could still swim in the Carioca River.

For me, the end of the world is OK. I'll soon be thickening up the soup of the dead. I'm young, in my fifties, but half a century is more than enough. My Cosme died when he was sixteen (fifteen?), I'm three times his age; I've had enough.

You know when you've got the flu, and your throat is inflamed? When you've got a fever and you're full of catarrh and feeling depressed and the over-the-counter medicine from the pharmacy is no help at all? When you suspect what ails you is something other than a cold or a virus, maybe something worse? Imagine living your whole life like that, always two or three notches below healthy people, always fearing the worst.

The worst, in my case, is much worse than yours. Two or three notches worse.

And in your case, of course, there'll come a time when you feel better. Just a few more days of rest, a few more doses of antibiotics.

I've always believed I didn't come into the world to be, but to have been, to have done. I was born posthumously. I was stillborn in my mother's arms, hanged by the umbilical cord, purple, almost plum; the doctor brought me around with mouth-to-mouth. My first kiss. I almost saved myself the trouble of being born. From that moment on, the stubbornness of blood kept me alive.

(In other words, if our species had to depend on the willingness of its members to stay alive, it would have bitten the dust a long time ago.)

Despite the disasters, I've had some good moments. My leg didn't improve over the years, but it never deteriorated to the point of immobilizing me, and I learned to walk with a single crutch, and these days a cane. I've had flus, suffered from aching bones, mouth ulcers, heartburn, gastritis, fungal infections. I don't need glasses, yet. Normal. I've taken correspondence courses and bought books, read widely, but I never went further than high school. I've had a lot of jobs: paper cutter, copy editor at a newspaper. I've always liked to draw, but never took it up professionally. I gave São Paulo a try, but came back to Rio. At my peak, I had an antique shop in the famous Cartago Arcade, in Copacabana. But I gave up the spot and moved out to Mesquita, where I lived until my mother died. With the money I inherited, I bought this apartment and another in Cachambi, which I rent out (R$1,150 per month + service charges and other fees; the tenant works for a bank). No one ever comes to visit.

Joana has three kids (two girls) who barely know I'm alive.

She's a journalist for a magazine and earns a good salary, but has never felt the urge to tell our story. She has better things to do.

She became one of those very tall, very skinny blondes who look potbellied because their posture is concave. Her children deflated her adolescent breasts and made the bags under her eyes puff up. Last time I saw her, about two years ago, it looked like she'd slept in a bath of bleach. She's old in the damp, flaccid way of someone who loved being young a bit too much.

10

"How old are you?" Joana, dangling upside down from a branch of the avocado tree, which Cosme was trying and failing to climb.

"Fifteen. Fourteen ...?"

Me, crippled at the foot of the tree, no way of going anywhere.

"Why don't you know? Didn't your mama tell you?"

"Dunno who my ma is."

Joana gave a broad smile:

"And your dad?"

I tried to stand up on my own, pushing my back against the trunk and using my staff for leverage, but couldn't manage it. Cosme lifted me up with a single tug, without looking, as though it were something we always did. For a moment I thought my sun-parched skin had lifted entirely from my flesh. It was the first time we'd leaned on one another.

"Dunno my dad either."

Until the day Dad went to get him, Cosme had been living with an old white woman in a little house in Barbacena. (Which is where his Minas Gerais accent came from.) That's what he told us. She'd looked after him for as long as he could remember—her name was Dora, Maria Doralina Trazim de Souza, but he'd always called her "Grandma" and the whole neighborhood did the same. His grandma told him that, as a baby, he was left on the steps of the Boa Morte Church, and then was passed from helping hand to helping hand, until he'd ended up in hers, the only ones that didn't want to let him go. She didn't know who his parents were. When he was naughty, his grandma told him she'd send him back to the priests.

The only clue left behind was a photograph, tucked into the folds of his baby blanket: thirty people posing on the wreckage of a crashed plane. I was fascinated by the image. It looked like the weight of the people had brought down the twin-engine plane, which lay with its nose buried, figures crowded on top of its wings and body. I don't know what happened to the photograph. Cosme only showed it to us once. I think he cut it out of a magazine, just to invent a story, and I believed it.

The fact is one day my father knocked on the door of the little house, had a coffee with Grandma Dora, gave Cosme a few affectionate slaps on the shoulder, and brought him to Queím. He would never leave.

11

My only friend is Grumá, my neighbor here in the building. José Grumari dos Santos, another one who's done everything and nothing with his life. A Vasco da Gama fan, with the face of an old sea dog. Fat neck and a jaw like a hippopotamus, barrel-chested and not too bright. A face wrinkled from the sun, the ponytail of a beach bum who's hung up his shorts. His house reeks of that sweet supermarket popcorn that is neither proper popcorn nor very sweet. He's about five years older than me. Says he was born in Ipanema, grew up in Madureira.

From time to time a pig dies an accidental death on his sister's farm. It might fall into an empty swimming pool and so need to be slaughtered and turned into bacon, tenderloin and pork chops, before ending up in Grumá's kitchen. He'll ask me to help him polish it all off. Flame-grilled, a squirt of lemon, beer, cachaça and crackling. The next day my guts will be on fire, because pork has never agreed with me. But these are the only times I get to see my next-door neighbor, when a pig meets an accidental end in Nova Iguaçu.

He once told me a story about a plane crash, which I'd also heard when I was a boy. In the 1940s, a plane came down somewhere near Pilares. On board was a baroness (sometimes Italian, sometimes Spanish and sometimes a countess), with her daughters and all the family gold, fleeing to Brazil to escape the war. It was a stormy night, and the small plane had limped all the way from Santos, which the ladies had reached on a ship that had a different name each time the story was told. The handful of people who lived in the area heard the crash and saw a flash of yellow lightning. Someone went to take a closer look. The guts of the little plane were split open and all the gold was spilling out, the burnt, bloody bodies spread on top in a last attempt to protect their fortune.

Men and women spent the entire night plundering the treasure. Bloodstained coins and tableware and jewelry were taken and buried throughout the region, including here in Queím. Buried because they could never be used. Cursed gold. "What kind of person would eat rice and beans bought with bloody gold?" Grumá asked me, chewing his rice and *farofa*. "Nobody. So it's buried all over and nobody knows where."

"So why did they take the gold?"

"Who wouldn't take it?"

The bodies were buried in the hills, along with the plane, so they say. On windy nights, when yellowy flashes appear over the mountains, Grumá says it's the golden ladies searching for what was stolen from them.

There's a documentary on climate change on the education channel. Another tsunami causing chaos in Asia. "Coastal cities such as New York, Guangzhou and Rio de Janeiro will suffer damage costing up to three trillion dollars ..."

Earlier, on the news, there was a story about two food vendors who stabbed each other to death on a patch of wasteland in Guadalupe in the North Zone. The vultures showed the families where the bodies were. The police only turned up after the journalists.

The law ends after Bridge 6 on Avenida Brasil, the gateway to the outer suburbs. Corruption too. The pure human is exactly that, a creature smart enough to invent the knife and draw from it the most obvious conclusion: murder. Corrupt are those who wrote the laws, because they invented crime. From that point on, it was the usual story: registrations, filings, rubber stamps, ratifications, office blocks, health insurance, guides to good conduct in the workplace, Kafka, traffic jams on Avenida Rio Branco, human resources departments. They invented every possible type of castration to put the brakes on our hunger for flesh. These days, a vulture is more of a man than man himself—citizen, employee, eunuch.

And this perpetual state of moral hangover.

(Though, at the same time, who wants to go through life starving?) (An office building can, at least, protect us from bad weather.) (A lukewarm love affair can even seem cozy.) (Believe in small kindnesses.)

13

They were running, I could hear the echoes snaking around the house. Joana's shrill laughter and flip-flops. Cosme's longer, heavier footsteps.

I tried to imagine what it must be like inside his brown skin, his locomotive tendons, steam from his mouth, blood pumping, eyes trained on his target, jaw clenched in concentration, his face playful but his body that of a serious predator. On corners, he'd put his hand on the wall for balance and to give himself a boost. His hands were enormous.

The two of them advanced, Joana the prey, Cosme giving her a head start because he wouldn't know what to do if he caught her—tickles, a hug, a trip, a bite? They raced past me and disappeared.

Dad was at home with us. It was the day my maternal grandmother died, but we only found out a week later, when Mama came back from her trip. I don't remember feeling sad. I'd never met her.

Suddenly, everything went quiet. Joana approached from one side, staring up at the ceiling in innocence. Cosme came from the other, slipping but quickly righting himself, gangly as a newborn fawn. "What happened?" I asked, and he replied, "Nothing," and repeated, nothing, and repeated, nothing, even though I hadn't asked again.

They hid inside until late. Late became morning and, shortly before lunch the following day, they came to me. Barely disguised panic on their faces. I was sitting at the edge of the pool, in the shade.

"Look," Joana said, and Cosme pulled dozens of golden shards from his pocket. They shone crazily in my eyes, as though the kid had a pile of tiny suns in his hands. He seemed resigned.

It was one of Mama's ornaments, a golden egg studded with tiny orange jewels. She collected these imitation Fabergés, which she displayed in a small, windowless room in the back of the house. Shelves and tables piled with fake gold eggs. With the lights off, the dim light was streaked a dull yellow.

I always hated that room. When Mama died, I threw almost everything away. I kept two or three of the little eggs.

Joana: "They'll send him back to the priests!"

A silence fell and echoed deep into my skull. I felt dizzy. My lungs, all of a sudden, choked up with acid. I wanted him gone, but I wanted him to stay. I didn't want to let go of my anger, but he was starting to grow on me. Fear, hate's smarter offspring, quickly gave me the idea:

"Bury it over there," I said, and Cosme closed his hands in surprise. "Bury it and forget about it. No one will notice."

14

The burden of burying her mother, the lonely funeral, the visions of the maggots to come, I'm not sure which it was, but my mother came back from that trip changed. The taxi—I've never forgotten it: a beige-and-black coffin-shaped VW 1600—pulled up at the gate, where all of us were waiting, including Cosme.

She got out of the car and said hello to the boy. Dad and Joana gawked. Before, she'd hardly given him a glance.

There was no affection in her greeting; she didn't hug or even come close to him, but that hello ignited my rage, which melted my eyes until I could hardly see. And then I was on the ground, my elbow scraped and my staff bouncing away after whacking Cosme in the face. A bubble of blood swelled in the corner of his eye, which turned to me without reaction. My scrapes were starting to burn, but I was just as panicked by his injury. I saw him go to put his hand to his wound, that he was about to cry out, but I heard nothing. I fainted.

And so the summer came to an end.

15

It wasn't just scrapes. I'd broken my arm. The strength with which I'd flung that piece of wood had dislocated my shoulder and, when my legs couldn't hold me up, I'd cushioned my fall with my hands. All my weight landed on that weak point. The bone popped out of its socket and snapped in two.

We rushed to the hospital, Dad and I, in the same taxi that had brought my mother home. On the way, he tried to push my arm back in place and shared a laugh with the taxi driver, "You've really done a number on yourself, haven't you, boy?" And he laughed, hawhawed, as though I'd won a baseball tournament. Who knows what it's like for a father to have a cripple for a son. It was eleven in the morning, and the sun was sucking the air from the car and my head.

I threw up everywhere.

That year, my nanny Paulina had a daughter she called Adriana (named after her husband, Adriano, who ran out on his family shortly after). When the mother's belly button was already a lump, Maria Aína read in the coffee grounds that the child would be unhappy, but wouldn't have time to experience true sorrow. She was right: Adriana had a child at the start of the century, when she was in her early twenties, but she died in childbirth.

The kid still lives in Queím. The day before yesterday I saw him in the middle of a litter of boys, twelve or so, all of them bare-chested (twelve shades of black), playing soccer in Bastilho Alley. As I passed on my way to the bakery, dragging my leg, he looked over. They all did—circus freak—but I recognized him. He's the spitting image of his grandmother.

I think he's called Renato.

His father was probably called Renato too.

My arm was in a cast for five weeks. My smothered skin, pale and always clammy, stinking of mold under the plaster, turned my stomach. When I came home from the hospital, my parents put me to bed. Mama took care of me, Dad popped in to laugh at his violent son, Paulina spoon-fed me lunch, Joana planted a kiss on my cheek to heal me.

And Cosme, had he died? I was afraid to ask Dad, terrified of going to jail and spending the rest of my life with the *bandidos*. He answered me seriously: no, but nearly. Where was he? Dad said we'd see each other soon, we had to make peace. I hung my head—right, make peace. I hated making peace (with my sister, with my classmates). Was it embarrassment, or unwillingness to shake my enemy's hand …? I no longer remember why. The truth is I was curious to see his face. I felt a tingling in my chest and further down. I wanted to see him because I wanted to see him. Was he badly hurt? Dad laughed no. Had it left a scar?

My hatred for him had vanished. If you ask me, in this world hate has the consistency of a cloud, a thing within the reach of anyone who wants to grab it, let it fester, and shape it however they want. It's an appendix of the mind. You can't own it, or aim it right, predict it or control it easily, it's a bubonic plague spreading, a runaway poison, lava from a volcano, the surf of a tsunami, I don't know what's the right comparison. After I walloped him with my staff, my hate no longer took Cosme's name or shape. And so, with a single blow, I began to love him.

18

Captain Bras had a barrel chest that would defy death itself. He was a fearless giant. A green-and-yellow bodysuit, a blue mask, a 100 percent Brazilian superhero I'd invented myself. The swordsman of liberty. Lying in Mama and Dad's bed, unable to draw (I'm right-handed), I reread the handful of pages I'd already made. The captain fought a monster made from a thousand cockroach shells: when he slew it with his sword, another creature crawled from its shell, the same but smaller. Our hero took a terrible beating from his foe and was on the verge of drowning in Guanabara Bay, but he would win in the end, he always won. I just hadn't drawn his victory yet.

His calves, I had a problem with Captain Bras's calves. They were difficult to draw, as were his pants and butt. A boy doesn't draw another boy's butt, a boy doesn't even look at, doesn't even think about the front of another boy's pants. I felt an anxiousness I couldn't put my finger on and looked for something else to read.

Among the pile of comics and books I'd been given to pass the time, I came across a magazine full of celebrity gossip, rumor and the misfortunes of TV and radio stars: WHAT KILLED MARLENE'S ENGAGEMENT? (I don't remember.)

Two photos of the couple at home, barefoot and relaxed. The two-tone oxfords of Paulo Farias, ex–future husband of the singer, placed casually in the foreground. The toes of Marlene Bernard, a minor star from the Tupi channel. Paulo's calves, snug in beige slacks. I began to feel the tingling below my chest again, descending to the lower part of my stomach. My penis awoke in little jerks.

When I looked, it had already escaped my pants. I closed my eyes, rolled onto my front, and, unable to use my right hand, squeezed it with my left. Until then, that was how I'd done it, on my stomach: I squeezed my dick and balls and rolled back and forth until I felt spasms in the depths of my pelvis. I hadn't yet ejaculated. These dry orgasms were the best of my life.

I'd project a variety of images onto the dark screen of my eyelids. I hadn't developed the butcher's craft of picturing only the parts of the body that would make me cum (feet/calves/butt/neck). Memories of school: Pedro's ankles as he ran after the ball, lanky Manuela staring at me from the other side of the playground, why did she stare like that? Did she want to see me with no clothes on? Paulina naked. All of it excited me because thinking about it was forbidden. The smell of sweat after PE class. I never took part. Cosme's dick inserted itself into the film. What would it be like? Fat and darker than the rest of his body. A tight ring of skin around the head. Would it foam? The boys at school said their dicks foamed, but mine had never foamed. Mine was slender, but long. Hard, it was the only straight thing on my body. Cosme. Cosme afraid of my dad. Cosme chasing after my sister, Cosme's big hands. My Cosme. If Manuela saw him, she'd want to marry him.

What really excited me was being in my parents' bed, the bed where I was conceived, and my sister too, where all the sex I knew about went on. The feeling of the forbidden grew, my stiffness too, there was a high-pitched whine in my head and suddenly that hot cramping in my stomach and a warm wetness in the palm of my hand. I opened my eyes, startled. It was the first time anything had come out. I thought I'd pissed myself.

Cosme was in the doorway watching me, shirtless, a half smile on his face. On his forehead, a small bandage, gauze and tape, made by Dad, I think just to scare me, because his injury looked much less serious than mine. He didn't jump when I jumped. He didn't blink as I squirmed and twisted, trying to pull up my pants. He kept on half smiling, that weird air of calm. I wiped the gooey cum on the sheets and waited. My shock swelled into fear, into terror.

He seemed to have become an adult overnight. His skin had darkened, his thighs had stretched. Hair. The smell of scrubbed flesh. His calves, once twigs, now tapered into broad, enormous, flat feet. My Cosme, terrible at soccer, always played center half. Useless for the army. He was a bit lopsided because the left side of his body looked more muscular than the right. The nipples on his slim chest, the color of figs. His voice was altered, deeper:

"What's that drawing?" and he came over to look.

(With that question, he accepted the apology I hadn't offered. Our peace was sealed.) A shiver along the hairs on the back of my neck. He came closer and closer. He put his right hand on my forehead and I felt how it was rough, warm. I don't know why he did that, and I don't think he did either. He stopped talking, stopped half smiling, turned and walked out, dragging his rubber flip-flops, his buttocks two engine pistons.

Then I remembered science class, and understood what had stuck my fingers together, what I'd wiped on Mama's sheets. I was struck by a callow fear: what if my mother rolled in it and got pregnant? I'd be my brother's father!

It was the only time I ever prayed.

God heard my prayer.

19

The two weeks that followed are deformed in my memory. Some parts confused, some things I can't place in time. Mama started smoking cigarettes that came in a golden packet. The first day of school was getting closer. One day, she packed her bags and moved to another house (a hotel?). The next day, she was back living with us, having forgiven my father. For what, I didn't know. Maybe he'd slept with his secretary? All men slept with their secretaries.

The two got divorced a few years later. Dad breathed his last in 1987, in a cabin out in Queimados, paranoid, demented, terrified they were going to put him in a tire necklace and set him on fire. The *bandidos*. Mama spent her last years penniless, in a one-bedroom flat in Taquara. Later still, when they were both dead, I discovered a little of the for what.

Gathering my mother's papers for recycling, I found a folder with my name on it. Inside, a letter and a few photocopied documents ("that the witness …"; "that the supposed doctor administered an injection"; "who heard the … who passed out from …"; "a substance that kept her awake for three nights";

"who answered to 'Doctor Pablo' and laughed when ...") that she'd received, probably, from one of my father's military friends. If it was all true (there were lots of official stamps, but I never tried to get to the bottom of it), Dad was "Doctor Pablo," who worked in the basements, making sure the tortured stayed alive. It might have been an invention of her bitterness. In the letter, Mama said she didn't know why or from where my father had rescued Cosme, but she thought he was the child of one of his victims, perhaps of his own rapist's seed. That was why she pitied the boy but couldn't bring herself to look at him, etc.—and that she loved me dearly and a kiss from your mother who loves you dearly ♥ ♥ ♥ Antônia de M. Cruz.

(Official stamps and history are easy to invent.) But if it was all true, Dad must be burning in the eternal pyre of witnesses that is hell. Or that's all rubbish, we die and disappear into the vacuum, our bodies become food for the trees and those who remember us die one day too.

20

Capital of Amapá? Macapá! The fans brought no relief, just wafted the hot air around the classroom. Forty kids and Miss Beth, a substitute, the germs making babies in our nostrils. When one of us got sick, we all did. Rashes were a team effort. Lice shaved the heads of all the boys at the same time. The girls couldn't do that, so had to douse themselves in medicated shampoo.

For my first few days back at school, my arm was still in a cast, and I had to be pushed around in a wheelchair. The pitying faces of the girls and the teachers, kinder than ever before. The boys tried to combine sympathy and respect in the same smirk. I was one of them now, a tough guy of unpredictable violence. The playground monitor let me go back to class late after break, I didn't have to copy anything from the blackboard, everyone signed my cast; life is sweet for a cripple with a broken arm.

I'm not nostalgic about my school days (São Sebastião, a private school, three blocks from my house, still exists), they were pretty dull. Good enough to learn to read, do sums, work out tax percentages and almost nothing else. I also discovered that the human fauna doesn't vary much. Lanky Manuela, for example (her surname was Pacheco Antino, I read in the yearbook they gave us at graduation), curly black hair, the domed forehead of a herbivore, from a Protestant family (she always had a Bible in her school bag). Skinny and flat-chested, shy and studious, she sat in the right-hand corner of the room, two rows from the teacher. Identical to thousands of other shy, studious lanky girls who sat in corners, near the teacher, in countless other classrooms across the five continents.

I'm certain my class could serve as a mold for every human being on the planet. The entire species could be summed up in those forty children (including myself), every tendency and temperament was represented. All the men, all the women, all the wars, all the enslavements and divorces and police forces, history in its entirety is there in embryo form. Humanity will go no further than these forty types. That's why I didn't keep in touch with any of my old classmates: I don't need to, I see them all the time. (Small world.) All of them more or less drawn toward, more or less distant from, the magnetic figure of the moment: at school, the teacher; at home, the parents; at church, the pastor; at work, the boss; on TV, the heartthrob; at the stadium, the star striker.

3	PRESENTE
4	FALTOU
5	PRESENTE
6	DOMINGO
7	FALTOU
8	PRESENTE
9	PRESENTE
10	FERIADO
11	RECESSO
12	RECESSO
13	DOMINGO
14	ADVERTIR

A.A. de C. ♂—Short-ass who got ugly in his teens, after being spoiled as a child. Compensated for it with relentless, forced cheerfulness. Really good at math. Front row.

A.B.M. ♀—Grew as strong as a boy, face like a dinosaur's mother, liked ball games (never martial arts). Sat in the back with the jokers, but still got decent grades.

A.G. dos S. ♂—Switched religion five times before he was eighteen. Liked to act like a holy hoodlum, but later straightened himself out. Today, he's the owner of a restaurant in a small country town.

B.C. e O. ♂—Fat and violent. Became nice later. Shared all the minutiae of his life, the notebooks and pens he liked the best, the food and drink, his bowel movements.

B.C.F. ♀—Considered the ugliest in the school. Sat in the front row, but couldn't get good grades. Started listening to jazz and liking avant-garde fashion, became sophisticated in Europe.

C.A.C. ♂—Me, crippled, shy and irritable. I sat in the left corner of the room, near the door (to make it easier to get out). Lost my temper when the teachers tried to help or give me special treatment.

C.B. das D. ♂—Friend to all, didn't drink alcohol until he was eighteen. The king of cheating and copying, he never got a bad grade. As soon as he could, became a family man. Abhorred physical violence.

D.A.C.A. ♀—Chubby and nasty. Showed off her rolls of fat like some show their middle finger. Lost weight in her teens, but not her aggressive personality, which came in handy in the workplace.

D.H. de M. ♀—Pretty little, prim little, pale little thing, virginal. The class queen.

E.A.A. ♂—Blond, a mini ladies' man, first to lose his virginity. Never worked out which path to follow, which would trouble him most, because it seemed like part of him was missing. Peaked at seventeen.

E.A. dos S. ♂—Smiled way too much. Everybody thought he was a bit simple or possibly a maniac.

E.V. ♀—Lived with her grandfather. Obsessed with caring for others, she became a nurse. Couldn't pass the university entrance exam for medicine.

F.A. da S. ♂—Rarely spoke, but every now and then couldn't contain himself and danced on the tables, took off his shirt, pretended he was scoring all the goals in the world, stuck his tongue out and waggled his head and laughed and hehhehed and hawhawed.

F.M.V. ♀—Shy, despite being well-developed. Acted like the much younger girls. When the kissing stage began, said it was just as well nobody wanted to kiss her, she didn't want to kiss them either, because it was unhygienic.

F. de N.I. ♂—Would swap a thousand cruzeiro notes for five, sometimes two, coins, because he thought change was prettier.

F.T.A.L. ♂—Nothing to make him stand out, until he got injured while camping. He was left with a scar that ran from his neck to his mouth. Everyone pampered him, which he accepted. Grew up believing people were kindhearted.

G.C. e O. ♀—Shape-shifter. Was, over the years, every character in *Scooby-Doo*: the scruffy, greedy skinny guy, the brave handsome one, the hopeless rich girl, the girl with the smarty-pants glasses, the cowardly dog. I don't know if he ever decided on one of them.

G. de A.P. ♂—Adored by his father, was never embarrassed to say he loved his friends. Would collect toy cars until the day he died.

G. dos S.V. ♀—A busty fake blonde from the age of fourteen. Dreamed of living in America and marrying an American. Let herself be filmed having sex and allowed it to be posted online (though at least filmed with a state-of-the-art camera).

I. de A.C. ♀—Poor but driven. Bettered herself in order to defend the powers that let her.

J.P.-C. ♂—Attempted suicide the first time he got dumped. A Pekingese, he barked loudly, and considered himself virile. Genuinely wanted to be a movie star.

L.D. de A.F. ♂—Kicked another boy in the head and was expelled from school.

L.S.S. ♀—Liked to draw creepy clowns. The first of us to learn to smoke and speak English, the first to get a tattoo. Sat in the second-to-last row. Thought she was freer than everybody else.

M.H. ♂—Once tripped me up because I didn't return his good-morning greeting. Then hugged me tearfully.

M.P.A. ♀—Lanky Manuela. Even today probably thinks God is great.

M.P. de I. ♂ —The first to have facial hair. Sweated, stank and accepted the disgustingness of biology. Tore shreds of skin from his fingertips and chewed them for hours because they were salty.

N.S. ♀—Never watched films unsuitable for her age. When they invented telethons, she donated. When they invented reality shows she voted. Pretty, a good student, extremely helpful and friendly.

P.C.B. Jr. ♂ —Beaten up in the locker room because he got a hard-on when the boys were showering. Had to switch schools.

P. da S.M. ♂ —Talk of cars led to the subject of girls, which led to the subject of money, which led to the subject of soccer, which led to the subject of cars. Worked tirelessly until he understood his schoolwork or until he retired.

P.F.C. ♀ —The only black-black girl in the room. Front row. Embraced her African roots: clothes, headscarf, hair, gestures.

P.R.Q. de M. ♂ —The kind of boy who becomes a systems analyst and writes three collections of poetry, never published.

R. de S. ♀ —Spiritualist and pure, God is the god in everyone. Liked only white things, got married and went to live in a penthouse in Barra da Tijuca.

R.E. da C. ♂ —Sprouted into a muscular teenager, enormous, almost deformed with strength, but was calm like certain giants from fantasy films. A gifted musician with a habit of driving very small cars.

R.S.X. ♀ —Planned to make a career out of robbing banks and starting the Revolution, but soon got addicted to cigarettes and *vinho verde*.

S.D. ♀—Daughter of Miss Beth. Rebelled furiously, over petty things, when everyone else no longer cared. Knew how to set her classmates against her own mother. Atheist and resolutely single.

S.S.K. ♂—White, a square face, brown topknot. Intelligent, almost. A natural leader, the alpha male of the class. Only able to give the orders because the front row didn't mind being ordered about.

T. de M. Jr. ♂—A blabbermouth, and slippery with it. Pointed the finger at troublemakers then hid the finger. When he grew up, became a bank manager and would have been a comrade in the Party if Brazil had been communist. Member of the nosy-neighbor police. Used to set the law on suspicious-looking blacks and hippies.

T.H.V. ♀—Always paid more attention to books than to her studies.

V. de A. ♂—Big-bellied at thirteen, married at seventeen. A decent sort. Faithful investor in the Brazilian dream. Savings account and time clock punched religiously, barbecue on Sundays to avoid thinking about death or the routine.

V.G. ♀—Seemed slightly broken by life, even when young. Wanted to get married and live in peace. To keep her friends, she made jokes about poo, or cabbage that caused wind, etc. Pigeon-toed.

They weren't sealed units, of course. Nobody is. They came together in gangs, tribes, packs, political parties, tea parties, pajama parties. Those who liked dogs and those who liked cats, subdivided into favorite breeds of dog and cat, etc. They were traversed by cold snaps and warm fronts, cattle stampedes, gut instincts and misunderstandings. Secret notes, fistfights, faces pulled behind backs, nicknames and smashed-up toys (once, G. de A.P. ♂ stamped on one of my model planes). They fought, conquered and were subjugated, engaged in every type of trade, including of the flu, infected each other and off they went. Each going their own way, each absolutely convinced they were the only chimpanzee destined for the presidency of Brazil.

Mama was a typical D.H. de M. ♀. Dad, it seems, was an L.D. de A.F. ♂. Joana is a rare case of an N.S. ♀ who transformed into a species of B.C.F. ♀ … I only know one person who didn't fit into any of the forty boxes: my Cosme. Him the world made, then broke the mold. The rest: boxable.

21

This morning, on the way to the bakery (at the Flower of Queím the third batch always comes out of the oven at 8:30) I again saw Renato, Paulina and Adriano's grandson, Adriana's son. White-and-blue state-school uniform, coffee-with-a-drop-of-milk skin, plastic Power Rangers backpack (for boys five years younger than him). I asked if he remembered me, he nodded, squeezed my hand, and ran off laughing loudly. I didn't have time to ask if he remembered his grandfather.

22

Queím is tiny, barely visible on large-scale maps, but when Cosme introduced me to the street (now I could play outside the house, I was a tough guy, for sure), the neighborhood grew so enormous in every direction that the air became thin. I choked (it was fear, for sure), and he patted me delicately on the back: "Everything OK?"

"Yeah."

"The street don't bite."

Avenida Suaçu, now Rua Enone Queirós. Boys kicking the

ball about like they kick it about today, one team shirts on, the other shirts off (or everybody shirts off), four flip-flops marking the goals. Cars honking warnings all the way from the first corner, so we'd stop the game without accidents or rows over disallowed goals.

Sometimes they'd lose the ball, and it would rise into the air, rise. Sun scorching the eyes. The ball would bounce: dust, dirt, bad concrete, dead cockroaches, manhole covers, the smell of stale beer, horse piss, from a mangy horse. And would land in the undergrowth of the slave house. The landscape faded yellow.

My arm was healed. I'd swapped back my staff for crutches, and was a full-time cripple once again, with my two metallic tentacles. Cosme came over and said "Let's go outside?" me "The pool?" him "The street."

A flash of panic: "Mama doesn't let me."

"Does so, she already said so, said you could with me."

Doubting him, I went to ask Mama, who growled a go away-away-away. She was hidden in her windowless room, polishing her fake gold eggs. She'd made up a bed in there, a single mattress, two pillows, silk sheets, a bottle of wine. Where was Dad? She shrugged.

The first thing I saw on the street was a woman. Black, skinny and pregnant, beige dress almost falling from her swollen breasts. Tearing handfuls of weeds from the ground (scraping her fingers with every snatch), the wondering expression of the mentally ill. Killing plants to pass the time. Cosme raised his eyebrows at me in sympathy: that one's mind is disturbed, she doesn't recognize a soul, she's living out a today that will never end. She didn't even have a name. No one knew who the baby's father was, and she didn't have the words to report the rapist. She died before giving birth, with her skull cracked open on the pavement. The next day, I saw the stain of faded blood, a brown ᣟ‚ᣟ-shaped splatter. Tripped, they said.

The second thing I saw on the street was a semicircle of people waiting for me. The whitest and youngest there, I was introduced to each in turn. Knots, skeletal, real name Norberto, was said to be a druggie (later they'd say he had AIDS blood like the singer Cazuza and was a faggot). He had the mannerisms of a skinny old woman, always sat with his legs impossibly crossed, double-knotted (hence his nickname), and smoked nonstop, one arm propping up the other in a Carmen Miranda gesture. Tiziu was blue-black, like the bird of that name, and had yellow teeth (three missing, crowded canines). His youngest sister, who was never there because she was pregnant. Otávio, who said I just had to speak to the god Omolu if I wanted to cure my leg. Porky, round as a barrel, who at soccer was only any use as a goalkeeper because he blocked the whole goal. There were around thirteen boys (and a few girls) in flip-flops, their feet dirty and calloused.

It was the first time I realized I lived among poor people. Maybe I was poor too? No. They soon made it clear I was different—different all-right-for-some, not different down-on-his-luck (which was a lot more common). I was very white, my sandals weren't rubber (they had Velcro!) and my house had a big gate and walls, nobody could see inside. Dad drove a Corcel and no one had ever seen my mother. Only a rich woman spent her life hidden like that.

"What does your dad do?"

"He's a doctor."

The silence of an oh.

"See?" Cosme said.

No one had believed it.

Report Card for COSME HENRIQUE DE SOUZA
Academic Year 1978
Term 1 Grades

Portuguese Language and Brazilian Literature: 6
Art: 7.5
PE: 4.5
History: 8
Brazilian Politics and Society: 5.5
Moral and Civic Education: 4.5
Math: 3.5
Health: 8.5
Natural Sciences: 8.5

FINAL GRADES

. . . . .

I've kept a stack of these documents of his, birth certificate (an authorized copy, father unknown, mother unknown, legal guardian: Maria Doralina Trazim de Souza), vaccination card, report card, things like these. What for? Maybe in the hope that something in them will explain the boy to me. He was terrible at math, but excellent at science, what's that meant to tell me? He knew what the force of gravity was. Is that meant to tell me something? He didn't like shoes, for example. When he could, he'd go barefoot, even in the filthy street. What's that meant to tell me? Once, he tore his right foot on a shard of glass, and ended up limping almost like me. For days he called me his twin. At night, hidden away in his dinky maids' room, he wept from fear of tetanus. It was Knots who told him what it was. Cosme didn't know he was vaccinated.

How absurd it is to try to write Cosme, Cosme's ways, Cosme's words, the faces Cosme pulled. How I wish I had a photo of him to stick in here. (I don't know if I'd have the courage.) He never even had an ID photo taken. Whenever I think about this, I find it incredible: almost every human being in history lived and died without having a single photo taken. My Cosme was probably one of the last.

(The police must have a photo of his prone corpse, his body covered in knife wounds, his face sunken.

Not one like that.)

24

There comes a time in a girl's life when she has to become a young lady. She starts to drip blood and bits of uterus down her thighs, and can no longer sit with her legs open, walk with her legs open, chew with her mouth open. She can't cough or sneeze without closing her mouth and has to keep it closed so as not to get fat or talk too much. A young lady doesn't laugh or speak loudly, doesn't play kids' games, doesn't interrupt whoever's talking, because she's a young lady now.

After Joana became a young lady, she shut herself away in her own world, which I imagined stank of menstruation, because she started to look at everything with disgust: at her mother, at me, at the streets and their inhabitants. She no longer ran, not even for sport. She spoke to me and Cosme too with a kind of repugnance, like she was doing us a favor. Her body stretched but remained boardlike and fatless. She clung to Dad because she loved him more than anything. When the time came, I stayed with Mama and she went to live with him in Queimados. (Later, she went to college, got married, tried to become a respectable lady or a doyenne of journalism, had

48

two daughters, got de-married. Her wide-open smile got rarer, then got rarer still, until I almost never saw it again. Adult Joana only smiled that way as a harbinger of bad news: firings, malignant tumors and deaths in the family.) I don't know how much she knows about Dad's history. I don't think she cares much about politics.

25

I was just wondering how long it had been since a pig died out at Grumá's sister's farm. And there he was at the door, ten o'clock in the morning, freshly shaven, cheap deodorant, hi-how's-it-going, could he come in (he was already on his way in), have a coffee? I've only got one cup, my own. I had to drink mine out of a *mocotó* jelly jar. He sat in the armchair and I took the wooden bench that serves as a sideboard. He smiled, looked around: "You've never asked me over ... Who's the kid in the picture, you?"

"No."

"Relative of yours?"

"No, no. Came with a bunch of things from a dead guy with no family. At the shop. Remember I told you about the antique shop? The one I had in Copacabana."

"Uh-huh ..."

"A lot of people die and there's nowhere for their things to go. Everything goes in the trash. Then somebody takes it and sells it to an antique shop. The whole lot for five or ten reais. I lost count of how many photo albums of lonely dead people I sold. There are people who buy them. There are people who like old photos. That one was left over when I closed the shop down. Nobody wanted it. I thought it was nice and had it framed."

"Right."

(*Pause*)

"No more pigs died out at your sister's place?"

"Not by accident, no."

So, he started to say "So …," he was after a little favor, an inconvenience, really, nothing much. He needed an oven, his had given up the ghost, he wanted me to pay for a new one in installments on my credit card, because his credit rating was rotten. "I'm filthier than Lula," and hawhawed. He'd pay it all back, he promised.

Lula hasn't been president for years, but Grumá is my only friend. How could I turn him down? I gave him my credit card and PIN, he went off to the mall and came back with the receipt. DW70 oven, six rings, dual voltage, white, autoignition, self-cleaning, sliding shelves: 12 × R$94.08, interest-free. Delivery in five business days.

He really did just buy the oven.

I love this boy posing alone, barefoot and small in this harsh world. He seems so defenseless, shirtless like that. I really don't know who he is, or when the photo was taken (it's not that old; the boy is probably still alive). You can't see his face clearly, but he looks to be smiling for the camera, or grimacing at the sun. He probably hates the sun, like me. In fact, if he had a piece of wood in his hand (at that age I could no longer stand without support), it could easily pass for a picture of me. We look alike: two white kids, singular, bodies shrunken amid the harshness of our surroundings.

26

Adriano came out of the move theater. We were sitting on the curb, Tiziu telling us how his aunt had died—in the shower, washing her belly button, which he pronounced "belly bitten" and which, if you poked it too hard with your finger, really would kill you. "Rubbish," retorted Iguatemi (Marcelo Pontes Iguatemi, a brown-skinned kid who went by his surname because he wanted to be a first lieutenant in the navy), sticking his index finger in his belly button to prove his point. Then Adriano walked by, shutting all our mouths.

He was thirty years old but looked fifty, because he spent the whole day under the accursed sun. He had the sour whiff of clothes sweaty for months and, on top of that, the sickening perfume of the long cinnamon sticks he always sucked. He nodded at us and walked off. This was Paulina's husband, the man who, in a few days, would kill Cosme. None of us knew him, he'd only nodded out of habit, to impose his presence.

We nodded back, full of fear.

(Who had the balls to joke that he was a dick sucker ...? Sorry, a stick sucker, a cinnamon-stick sucker, haw! Nobody. Nobody had.)

He'd come from the Maier Cinema, about three blocks from

our street (the building is still standing: it's become an evangelical church). Had he been to see *Superman*? *The Other Side of Midnight*? Were Tom Mix, *Mandrake the Magician* or *Flying G-Men* showing at the time? In Queím, it's more than possible. Would he have eaten popcorn? Hard to imagine killers eating popcorn, or with caramels stuck in their teeth, laughing the sparkling, goofy laugh of the movies … The killer loved the movies. He always had a cinnamon stick in his mouth. Or I invented him like that afterward, always chewing a cinnamon cigar.

I must have invented it. We can convince ourselves of anything. For example, Gestas—Alfredo Gestas, the Queím ripper (I don't know if anyone remembers him, or if he's well-known outside the North Zone, outside Rio; he was in the papers a lot in the 1980s)—who invented that he'd killed a man. He was fixated on it: he'd killed a tramp with a hammer, chopped him up and disappeared with the body. He was able to reconstruct this memory down to the tiniest details, how the light fell crookedly on the pool of blood, the waves of adrenalin, the moment of revelation every first-time killer has, the grimace of the victim and everything else. He believed so strongly in his own invention that he ended up convincing the police. Life imprisonment. Months later, they discovered that Gestas had invented even the victim, a homeless person with no official papers. He was transferred to a secure psychiatric unit, condemned to life internment. In the asylum, when he was more or less lucid, he begged to be sent to the electric chair. He died with that guilt. It was plastered all over the front pages.

I've always wanted to believe, deep down, that I'd be able to convince myself I'd invented all of this, invented Cosme and the death of Cosme, my nanny's killer husband, my father the angel of torture. That this entire world is no more than a delusion of my crippled mind. That another such world is possible, one almost identical (with my bad leg, with Queím and everything, Brazil, poverty and tragedy, no problem at all), but a little less heinous.

Or, if not less heinous, a little more varied. I once read in a poem that we're "dolls of hardened lava / and it's with tears they mold us." In the poem, called "Chicago, 1999," a salary-man remembers all of a sudden that there are volcanoes in his country. It really is the type of thing we forget, thinks the man in the poem, until one erupts.

Never has anyone said anything like this to me, even the poet who wrote this poem wouldn't have said a thing like this in ordinary life. So it's ordinary life that has to die; my Cosme died in ordinary life.

27

Before all this concrete, most of the streets in Queím crackled with little round stones, souvenirs of a branch of the Carioca River that ran dry around here. They were never any bigger than marbles, the big ones. The colors: brown, beige, milky white, gray or cloudy ice. The games I remember most fondly were invented with these pebbles, scavenged from the road for free. To start with, I copied well-known games—checkers, solitaire, come-and-go, Battleship—or made up distortions of more complicated games, like chess or backgammon. Later, still using the boards I had, I'd make up new rules. Later still, new boards.

The game I was trying to teach Cosme that day was my masterpiece. I don't remember the name, I only know it was played with lots of small black stones, which were the ordinary people, and a few stones from each common color (gray, beige, milky white, brown), which had power over the black ones (to kill the nearest stone, for example, or switch sides). And two cloudy stones (the rarest), which were the players. The goal was to kill your rival.

There was no board. Or rather: the field of play was the house, the neighborhood, any place, any little corner! I explained, trying to stir up my friend's interest. We were in my room. He was trying to keep up, yawning a few questions. But weren't it hard, huh? All this adding, multiplying, measuring with a ruler, reading rules and forms (five notebook pages alone … both sides!), boring stuff for a game, weren't it? Sounded like school. More fun would be lining up the stones, half on each side, and flicking them at the enemy. As I was about to explain that, yes, there was a stage when the stones, and there were lots of them, hit each other, Dad came into the room. He was drunk, and stumbling slightly, like his crippled son.

He was carrying a tray of cheese buns. I asked him where Mama was; he wrinkled his nose to say he didn't know. He slurred out a few somethings. Wanted to know how his boys were. He gazed at the stones tenderly, yes, tenderly. A battle, I was about to explain, but Dad blurted that he loved us, right out of the blue, and that we should eat. Cheese buns? he offered up the tray.

We didn't have time to take it. He blew out a high, long "ee" like a puncture in a balloon. His eyes staring.

He was crying, but without tears. Dry sobs, snorts from his nose, wordless Dad, staring at us with that milky-white face cry-smiling (he'd gotten fat, his gray beard was a few stiff shoots on his sagging skin), his eyebrows wrinkled into a ∧. He scrunched up his face to squeeze out a few tears, but the tears wouldn't come. His eyes weren't even damp, only lusterless. They looked like two wads of cotton, the ones they put in the nostrils of the dead. Now, who'd be brave enough to take the first cheese bun?

He put the tray down and lay on the bedroom floor. Right on top of our stones, which went click-clocking everywhere, scratching the wooden floor. Drunk, he didn't even notice them digging into his flesh. (In any case, he was used to it: he was born and grew up in Queím, on the peanut-brittle ground around here.) He rolled onto his side, curled up like a conch or a snail shell, and hugged himself. Me and Cosme sat frozen amid the scene, my nearly old dad contorted from sadness, shriveling up, a fat man shriveling up with pain on top of the tiny pebbles.

I lay down too and curled back into his arms, which embraced me gratefully. I said something consoling, I don't remember what, which unstoppered his sobs. I felt his choking breath on the back of my neck, an och-o-ohh from the depths of his esophagus, desperate with relief. The tears finally came, and the phlegmy hiccups, the sloppy cries of mercy, his big gut massaging my spine.

Cosme sat where he was, looking on in wonder.

A friend of his had died. Hiccup. He'd had to identify the body. Hiccup. There must have been plenty of corpses in my doctor dad's memory, but this one had knocked him sideways: gunshot to the back of the neck, at point-blank range. Smell of blood and burnt hair. Hot breath of alcohol mixed with the perfume of cheese buns. He'd been a minor administrator in a government department, a friend from childhood. No enemies or debts, let alone a mistress. My father was his only actual-friend friend. Wife inconsolable. No children. They'd ditched the body in scrubland out in Recreio.

Because? Because no reason at all, no one knew why. Could be he dropped a business card on the bus, a maniac found it and decided to pursue him to death. Could be they robbed him for small change and killed him for the fun of it, for the taste of it. These days they killed over nothing, a man's life was worth nothing, was worth less and less each day. After all, there were too many people on the planet (5 billion!), one more, one less, what's the difference? I reached for a cheese bun and ate it furtively. Cosme too, and we smiled, accomplices. Dad squeezed me, because his sadness was powerful. I felt his hip bone against my back.

28

The ants had eaten his eyes.

"Whose?"

"The dog's. Eaten everything, only the holes were left."

They were playing adventures, Cosme, Iguatemi and Zetimó (short for José Timóteo; him I didn't know so well). They sneaked around the neighborhood, scraping their thighs on the rough walls, crawling into other people's gardens, whispering in code and imagining the things that kids imagine: Iguatemi that he'd fought for his country in a war, Zetimó that he was hunting for pirate treasure, Cosme, I don't know, maybe just keeping his friends company. I wasn't with them, of course, I heard the story later, from Iguatemi.

The tale was that they found a dead dog in the back garden of Senhor Arturo, a cranky, leathery Spaniard, Moorish, almost brown, who lived beside the old slave house. The dog wasn't his, but it had decided to die there in that garden, because why not, because dogs can die where they want. The old man thought the kids had hit the animal with their catapults (they always carried catapults, for duels to defend their honor and monster slaying) and made them move the body. But, Senhor Arturo, that thing has been dead for ages, it's even a bit stinky, look. That to him—Arturo—sounded like a lie. But, Senhor Arturo, move it where? Not his problem. The killers would find a way.

"And what did you do?"

Cosme did it. He grabbed the dog by a hind paw and dragged it to the waste ground at the slave house. He ordered us to start digging. We dug, with our bare hands. (Iguatemi showed me his dirt-stained fingernails.) Then he put a foot on the dog's belly and yanked hard on its front paw, ripping its whole leg off in one go. The corpse had hardly any blood left in it, it was stone dead. Next, he tore off the other three legs, each more furiously than the last, without even a grunt. He couldn't cut off the head—he'd need an ax!—so kept stepping on the neck to see if it had loosened, kicking the skull like he was taking a free kick. Nothing. He gave up and came to help dig. We buried the body and legs in the same grave.

Problem solved.

That's what he said: "Problem solved." Iguatemi looked at me with the nervousness of a navy captain who's never seen war. How do you do a thing like that? With no sympathy or pity…

29

The sun rises behind the slave house, it always did. At eight o'clock on a Sunday morning (why were we awake, me and Cosme? And already outside?), we walked by it. In the small hours of the night there'd been a celebration for Omolu, the god of smallpox. The scrub had been trimmed. A few colored cloths hung from the branches of a tree and billowed out into the center of the prayer ground, where their ends were fixed to the top of a post. The post was bedecked with ears of corn, half-rotted persimmons, sprigs of fragrant leaves and black, red and white ribbons. Surrounding it, wooden chairs. In one sat Maria Aína, dressed all in white, the hem of her dress smeared with mud.

Backlit by the sun, the old woman was resting her legs before returning home to get some sleep, finally. She was smoking a pipe, something I'd never seen her do before. A few young women, also tired from lack of sleep, collected the clay serving dishes and kept an eye on the embers on the ground, so they wouldn't ignite and start a new fire. You could still smell the beans, the aroma of the palm oil, of the rue leaves. Scattered over the prayer ground, the leftovers from the feast: white corn pudding, red corn with onions and molasses, popcorn, lots of popcorn spilled in the mud.

(Years later, I learned that at festivals for Omolu there was always some poisonous food hidden among the real thing. You had to know which was which. But in Queím no one died, at worst they were confined to bed for a few days.)

My Cosme was nervous. He tugged my wrist, he wanted to get out of there fast. I grabbed his hand, our fingers intertwined. The sun climbed up our faces.

I wasn't feeling like myself either. A rage in my blood, born out of puberty, told me to be careful. Those women could kill us at any moment, lacerate our flesh, cook and eat it with pink corn paste. Even at that hour, exhausted, with the old slave spirits and the *pombajiras* already far away, back in heaven, in hell, in Aruanda, there's something about women, a threat. I don't know, something about the uterus. How was I supposed to know? We were scared.

Maria Aína got up and walked stiffly toward us. She looked like a malnourished ox, with bones poking against her flesh. A fright. We untangled our fingers (shame at holding hands for so long, the hands of sweethearts). She smiled with her eyes shut. She knew everything before anyone else.

She didn't follow any saint, she no longer channeled the spirits because she didn't need to: she already had one foot in their world. She came very close, almost brushing her whiskers across my face, and breathed pipe smoke into my eyes. I felt a stinging blindness. It was then that she said she liked me and loved me as her son, because I was born just like her, hanged by the umbilical cord: "Anyone born that way will always be on the edge of trouble, *ossí*." My eyes filled with tears.

Cosme stammered a question. Maria Aína replied, gazing at me:

"Things don't need us people, *dejú*."

I don't know what he asked, I didn't hear. I've been trying to think of a question that fits perfectly with Maria Aína's answer ever since, but to this day I haven't found it. Basically, any one will do.

Three days later, Maria Aína was dead from natural causes. She left children, grandchildren, great-grandchildren, great-great-grandchildren. Forcibly transplanted to Brazil, her fearsome dynasty didn't end in the 1970s. Beautiful Maria Aína, my black grandmother. They didn't let me go to the funeral, I, who was practically a grown man, cried shut up in my Cosme's room, the former maids' room.

30

It was all a lie. It wasn't that Maria Aína was trying to fool us. She had nothing to gain from that. The *filhas de santo*, the entire religion. It wasn't out of bad faith. But in truth any answer works, it's we who'll never understand the question. The prayer ground at the old slave house: a lie. The trances, the old slave spirits speaking in Yoruba Portuguese: an elaborate lie, decorated with ribbons and persimmons, stuffed down the gullet with flan and molasses. We do what we can.

I remember: Cosme was so scared. He badly wanted to talk to the saints and find out the future, because deep down he knew that nobody, not even they, could find out his past. What he had was a terrible dread that one day they'd tell him his fate was to die in an accident. He didn't want to die in that way or from violence. He didn't want the danger of being crippled, of losing a leg. Dying from disease, though, that would be fine.

31

The boy is here at home, at last, Renato, son of Adriana, grandson of the killer. He came because he wanted to. I passed him on the corner by the bakery and asked if he wanted to come home with me. "What for?" but he didn't wait for an answer. He was alone, he had nothing better to do, he shrugged his shoulders and "C'mon." He gave himself up without many whys, like those poor girls who, even with plenty of pride and self-respect, give themselves too easily to men (a thing my sister, for example, would never do. Dad had money. Money buys whys, and modesty).

Now he's over there, napping on the bed I made up: a sleeping mat, pillow and quilt on the living room floor. The door is unlocked, he can leave whenever he wants. But he isn't the least bit scared of me. Earlier, I made a snack (hot dog and chips) and he complained that I only had the crusty rolls, didn't I have the soft hot dog rolls? And no Coke? And no sweet buns?

While the kid ate (he has the disgusting habit of drinking while he's chewing, to soften the bolus), I asked him some questions. He lives with another child (Carla, fourteen, no father or mother either) in a lean-to at the home of the girl's aunt (Anunciação, age unknown), a friend of his mother Adriana's, who adopted him because that's what women do. This aunt is out of the house all day, sometimes she doesn't even come home at night, lots of nights.

His mother? He doesn't remember. His father vanished off the face of the earth after he was born, just like his grandfather. What was his name? Renato like you? He didn't know. His great-grandfather probably abandoned his family too, and his great-great-grandfather. The kid is part of a long line of men who ran out on pregnant women.

How old? Ten, almost eleven.

Rough skin. Big hands, square jaw. A prime example of the evolution of *Homo sapiens*. It was in the paper the other day: scientists discovered that the human face was formed to withstand punches. We have this face because the species spent millions of years getting beaten up. Our hands have this shape because they evolved to make fists and dish out beatings. Renato sleeps with his fists slightly clenched, his guard up, his jaw restless.

I'm going to sleep too.

I'm going to lie down next to him.

32

When I woke, around eleven o'clock, the boy had gone. I don't know if he spent the night here and didn't have the heart to wake me to say goodbye or if he escaped in the middle of the night, revolted by my crippled body next to him. There's a fierce sun outside. ∴ It's been ages since it rained. (Or no, no, it rained the day before yesterday.) Sleeping on the floor has left me all seized up.

Grumá put an envelope in my mailbox. Inside, nine R$10 notes. It's the payment for the first installment of the oven—which on my credit card bill is R$94.08 per month. He rounded it down. If he keeps this up for the next eleven installments, he'll take me for R$48.96. He didn't even have the decency to write a note, nothing.

I don't know why, but the memory just came to me that, when beer bottles are ice-cold, he calls them "builders' calves." The grayish-white ice looks like cement dust on the cinnamon-brown glass.

I also recalled: once his mother, already an elderly senhora of eighty, saw Renan Martim on the beachfront in Copacabana. He's an actor who back then played a pure-blooded villain in the eight o'clock soap opera. The old lady went up to him and, rejuvenated by rage, headbutted him in the kisser! Broke her glasses and everything. The guy's teeth scratched her forehead. He was left a bit woozy.

When people from the beach asked why she attacked him, she explained the mischief this Martim had gotten up to. The blood running down her face. And worse: she'd read in a magazine of a bad deed, a terrible deed, a truly horrendous deed to come. But doesn't senhora know it was a soap opera? She knew—of course she knew, she wasn't gaga, she wasn't an idiot. She hated him anyway.

I've never forgotten this story. Grumá's mother hated with a hatred capable of effortlessly passing through every layer of the world.

33

There they were again. Playing soccer after class. Four-a-side, everybody with their shirts off, the street closed from corner to corner, two pairs of Kichute cleats for goals. Me, in the shade of an awning, keeping time on the clock (two fifteen-minute halves) and the score. I couldn't play, but I liked to watch, predicting the dribbles, the runs, the shoulder barges, the whole awkward ballet. From time to time, I'd decide if there'd been a foul or not. And I could always tell where they were going to kick the ball, who was going to take out whose leg, I was good at guessing the moves.

Anyone who thinks the cripple knows nothing about the furies of the body is dead wrong. It's we, the lame, the malformed, the amputees, the obese and the minuscule, the allergics, the hemophiliacs, the hemiplegics, the para-, tri- and tetraplegics, the dwarfs, the albinos, those who always have the flu, the entire legion of individuals saved from natural selection by human compassion, it's we who understand the glory of muscles and tendons, the minutiae of changes of temperature. (So many times I'd imagined playing soccer, getting into fights, chucking a stone through a window!) The healthy body we lack has been remade so many times in dreams that we're capable of inventing a new body, a body beyond, a body beyond beautiful, a body of Christ, but with skin so taut the crown of thorns :‘: wouldn't wound it and the nails couldn't perforate it. Imagine how much more beautiful the *David* would have been if Michelangelo hadn't had arms. And the *Venus de Milo*.

A toe poke from Knots in the direction of the goalkeeper. This shot went askew. The ball exploded red on Otávio's chin, his head went back, down he went. When they went to look, his mouth was full of blood. He'd bitten his tongue, but made a gesture to say it was nothing, it was nothing, all his teeth were in place, let's play on. He spat, considered his blood on the concrete. Cracked a bloodstained smile. Someone offered a hand and he pulled himself up, his sweaty belly creased into what little rolls of fat he had. Chests and bellies brushed in a quick hug, arms, slaps on shoulders, drops of sweat and on with the game. Oh, the skin. Go on, you useless shithead! Calves and eyes. The dry whine, the whimper, of the kicked ball.

Goal from Iguatemi, on Otávio's team, through the legs of my Cosme, the worst center half in the world. 7–3.

Iguatemi, the star player, military posture, concave stomach, chest puffed out. In the social strata of the neighborhood, he came just below me. His dad was a civil servant: his own house, an old car but nothing ever lacking for the kids. The others teased him when he turned up all groomed or when he put on airs, as if the armpits of his white T-shirts didn't turn yellow like everyone else's.

I met up with him again around ten years ago. We went for a beer, both of us half-reluctantly, just to not disrespect the it's-been-forever. Turned out he hadn't made it into the navy. He'd gotten fat and grown lumps, like Senhor Arturo the Spaniard, a skin like wrinkly ginger. He explained it was an illness. Explained he'd never married. He'd lived with his mother until she died and after that, and after that, and after that. Now he could only screw whores, he no longer knew how to talk to regular women. He talked about TV, the news, he talked about politics. For Iguatemi everything was rotten these days, they had to shut it all down and start from scratch. But Brazilians were a dumb breed. What the country needed was a good old-fashioned civil war. He talked about soccer too, but he didn't talk about that day. (A typical T. de M. Jr. ♂.) A sideways hug goodbye, promises to arrange another beer. He's probably dead now.

The match ended 9–5 for Otávio's team, six goals by Iguatemi. Knots was the top scorer on the other team, with four goals. Nobody could stop Knots either, he sneaked through the center of the defense and, face-to-face with the goalkeeper, just had to knock it past him.

Afterward, they came and spread themselves in the shade around me. The happiness throbbing in their legs, the salt on their lips. Heads dizzy from effort and pleasure. The heat of the eight bodies was a single mass of hot air that hovered a few inches from the ground and entirely coated us all. Suddenly they roared with laughter, and loudly remembered a move, huh-huh-huh, did you see it, Camilo? I'd seen it all. Right between the legs. The smell of wholesome sweat. The healthy ones.

And various subjects: Iguatemi's father had bought a TV and Porky's mother had won on the *bicho* (an ostrich ticket: number 1404; I remember exactly), she was thinking of getting one too. What, everybody's going to have a TV now? Tiziu said he'd never be able to buy a TV. Another subject: Tiziu's sister big-bellied from pregnancy, maybe with twins or maybe with a gigantic monster. What color was a baby's poo? Brown? A brown most like whose skin? And they all put their arms in a circle to compare. (I don't remember what was decided.) Afterward, a long discussion about the differences between air bombs, bangers, firecrackers, bang snaps and caps.

Had anyone there been to a brothel yet? Hahas.

Did anyone know that Adriano guy?

I said I did: he was Paulina's husband. To try and guess more about him, we described his features again, his way of walking, the cinnamon sticks forever in his mouth, always going to the movies, looked like he never took a bath, looked like the explorer Pedro Álvares Cabral—Cosme said, his face like a philosopher. He looks nothing like him! Fuck's sake, Cosme you dickhead, who knew what Pedro Álvares Cabral looked like?

The cloud of heat didn't seem to want to cool down.

It was strange to see how our friends from the street treated Cosme. Sometimes they'd throw sand at him for a joke, trip him up, call him an ass, all laughingly, and he took it all laughing. I don't remember seeing serious fights between them, they never made jokes about my friend's orphanhood, but they took him for an almost inferior animal, especially when it came to soccer and women. I knew in that gang he wasn't the leader, but at home he was the only young, healthy male, everyone respected him. Seeing him getting pushed around by smaller kids tied my chest in knots. Almost like that scene in *The Bridges of Königsberg*, the only thing I remember from the film: a boy walking through the city with his father. They're on one of the bridges when the father runs into the boss of the department where he works. The boss humiliates him, shouts at him, slaps his hat—for no good reason, I think just because they're in front of the boy.

The father doesn't react.

34

The boys were no longer soaked, the sweat had dried to a fine salt, covering the brown and black skins with a layer of whitish powder. The cloud of heat that had surrounded us, given off by those same bodies, dissipated slowly, making room for the nonhuman, airier heat of the street. From time to time, one of them would shiver all over with chills. We were close to one another, but no one had said anything for a few minutes. We were crocodiles after lunch, bloated in the shade, almost not seeing the point in so much existence.

Knots, lying back, his legs double coiled, lit a cigarette. He blew smoke upward, sultanesque. I was a little afraid of him. (I remember this is what I thought of him at the time: that he'd be capable of breaking his wife's fingers with a hammer, of throwing me in a river filled with crocodiles in Barra, of booting a dog right in the ribs. But no, Knots was a sweetheart. He later became a nurse. Today he works in Bonsucesso General Hospital. Confirmed bachelor. A typical E.V. ♀.)

Without a word, Otávio got up and walked off in the direction of the old slave house. Zetimó followed, Cosme went after him. I went too, without knowing why. We all went, apart from

Knots, who went home: he knew what was going to happen and was already too old for it.

I know it was afternoon, but I remember it as night or as if we were in a dense shade, green. Humid forest. Eight boys in a circle, in a corner of the old slave house, dicks out, cigarettes extinguished in our mouths, comparing sizes, thicknesses … Flying bugs, forest. Dragonflies? I don't remember dragonflies. Haziness. Chill. Forest, molasses grass. Amid the whispers someone struck a match. Every now and then, a few slaps on their own thighs and necks to kill insects. This was a miniature Amazon: earth, trunks, moss and climbing plants: forest, sand, steam, twigs, slime, delicate flowers. A giant forest, entangled branches and vines—all piled up like the toy castle of a child god.

I barely know the name of a single animal, but there was an insect that made a noise like a cicada and wasn't a cicada, it was the buzz of a propeller, a one-inch single-engine plane. Beetles, ladybugs. There were fireflies too, but these are almost gone today. Skunks, mice, earth cockroaches and sewer cockroaches.

Zetimó and Iguatemi heard a noise and broke the circle, jumping sideways, dicks out and everything. From nowhere Iguatemi had a machete in his hand, Zetimó giving him cover, staring straight ahead, skipping like a boxer.

Fsst, fsst: Iguatemi tore twice at the earth, disturbing the dry foliage. The thing was still moving under the leaves and the kid sliced up the entire ground.

Zetimó went and grabbed it: it was a cobra, now without a head and a piece of its tail, dripping blood. Neither was the type of man to be scared of cobras, they were experienced killers, dicks dangling, looking at us as though in an end-of-fishing-trip photo. Low applause, muttered congratulations.

The corpse of the cobra was thrown far away.

Back to the circle, silence. The fingers and fists started to move, pulling foreskins, the soft heads hardening; how it must hurt, I was thinking. Fake moans. We were accomplices in the purest crime, a crime unsullied by anything, the most immaculate crime of all. Drags, coughs (no one knew how to smoke, only Knots, who was the oldest, but he refused to teach us).

I watched, confused, I didn't do it like that. But my Cosme came to the rescue. "Look," his face whispered, and he showed me how, hold it like this and move your hand. How had I never thought of this? Pull the little bit of skin! And before I'd started someone had already cum. Two, five little drops soon drunk by the black earth. It was Otávio, who pulled up his pants, turned his back and went off smoking but not inhaling, without a word.

One by one we came and off we went, not saying a word. The whole thing didn't last more than six minutes.

This was almost forty years ago. Every time I pass in front of the old slave house, I remember the silence. Of course we never spoke about it, but that quiet orgasm sealed our friendship.

I was also drunk by the black earth.

The next day, they updated the score. Iguatemi: 433 snakes killed; Zetimó: 297 snakes killed; the rest: zero snakes killed. The more colorful the snake, the more poisonous it was.

35

My Cosme has been losing his features over time. I no longer remember clearly what his face was like, just a few broad lines, a few pieces reheated a million times in the imagination: his face when he tasted unsweetened lemonade, the grimace of the first time. A tired smile at the end of a pick-up game. Eyebrows in dead neutral on a boring afternoon. His predator's eyes chasing

Joana. The solidarity on his lips when he taught me how to cum … I've recalled these memories so many times that now what I see is no longer my friend's face of flesh and cartilage, but a worn-out image, buried under fourteen thousand re-rememberings. And even that indistinct face is disappearing in the froth, a hippopotamus snout half sunk in muddy water. (I've never seen a hippopotamus, not even at the zoo. Only on TV.)

What a gap a photo leaves.

Yesterday I dreamed about him. The face was recognizable, but older, riddled with dark wrinkles, but he was pregnant, heavily pregnant, just like Tiziu's sister. Twins. We had sex, he on his side, caressing his belly, he looked bored. Or else it was nausea. Or it was rancor because I hadn't kept an old promise. He was dry and hurt me. We lived together in Jacarepaguá, in a gray-and-yellow square. Pitiful trees, because the roots only sucked up water from the sewers. Houses behind fences. I loved my Cosme like you loved your first love, who was called Bruno or Pablo or Ilyich, Ricardo or Rhana, Luciano, Eduardo, Diego or Carlos Octávio, Kátia, Mariana, Lucas, Marisa or Carlos Eduardo, Rafael, Raí or Solange, or Luíza, Fabiana, Adolfo, Lígia, Joana, Érica, Mateus. Loved him like Lucas loved Sophia and Daniel loved Gabriela. Like Denilson loved Raiane, like Aline loved Michael, like Raquel loved Guilherme, who died of meningitis. Like Dimitri loved Cristina or Estefânia, like Lucas loved Ana Carolina and Ana loved Murilo. Like Carolina loved Victor, Marília loved Leonardo, Rodrigo loved Amanda, Marcelo loved André, Nathalia loved Rodrigo, Marianna loved Cadu and Laura loved Antoine. Like Fernando loved Clarissa and Daniel loved Gustavo, like Thiago loved Diego and Domingos loved Inês, like Leandro loved Cynthia and Marcos loved Daisy, like Sylvio loved Maria Beatriz and Júlia loved Fernando, like Sofia loved another Fernando, whose nickname was Xina. Like Cecília loved Natanael and Mirna, Jean. Like Matilde loved Maria and Fabiano loved Suzi, like Dinah loved Cláudio and Carla loved Ademar. Like Franklin loved Leônia, like Rodrigo loved Flora, like Guilherme loved Thiago, like Luca loved Ana, like Aparecida loved Renato. Loved him like Felipe loved Gabriela, Mauro loved Olívia, like Felipe Augusto loved Pedro, like Natália loved Juan. Luciane loved Jefferson and Otávio loved Rui like I loved my Cosme. Ana loved Rodrigo like I loved my Cosme. Danilo was loved by Mayara, Luis was loved by Lorena, Vinícius was loved by Ana Luíza and Théodore was loved by Eugénie like I was loved by my Cosme. Roxana loved Eduardo, Renato loved Roberta. Jorruan loved Késsia, but it was a platonic love. Jorruan loved João. Julia loved Gabriel, Giovani loved Alan, Patrícia loved Elisabete like I loved my Cosme, like Márcio loved Gilsinho and Tarik loved Ana. Cristina loved Xan, Roberta loved Marcus Vinícius, Graziela loved Paulo, Isabel loved Felipe, Maria loved Anselmo. I loved my Cosme. Karina loved André, Luis Felipe loved Joaquim, Guilherme loved Marianne, Leonor loved Marcos, Pacelli loved Erick, Amanda loved Maíra. I loved my Cosme. Sandra loved Luís, Jean loved Aloísio, Ricardo loved Sara and Isabella loved Victor, the author of this novel. I loved my Cosme like Bárbara loved Guilherme, like Johnny loved Mariana, like Douglas loved Ana, like Gustavo loved Raquel, João loved Victoria, Eudes loved Gilberto, like Kamila loved J. Luiz, like Diego loved Olímpio, like Paulo loved Isabel, like Gedion loved Renié and Tiago loved Jéssica. I loved my Cosme. Like Jeannie loved Murilo I loved my Cosme. Like Márcio loved Gustavo I loved my Cosme. Like Mariana loved Adriano, like Camila was loved by Glauber, like David loved Lele, like Raíssa was loved by Otávio. I loved my Cosme like Juliana loved Laura, like Melissa loved Tales and Guilherme loved Dolores. Kemy loved Felipe, Ellen loved André, Amanda loved Fábio, Mariano loved Joana like I loved my Cosme. Clarissa loved Rafael, Alice loved Bernardo, Daniela loved Ricardo, Thiago loved Natália, Priscila loved Andreas, Diogo loved Luciana, Leonardo loved Ícaro like I loved my Cosme, for the first and only time. Marília is loved by Leonardo and I love my Cosme. Sérgio loved Greice, Julia loved Leonel, Pedro loved Maurício, Luiz loved Ana, William loved Karina, Mariana loved Paulo, Leonardo loved David. I love my Cosme. Isabela was loved by Diego, Pedro was loved by Julia, Luís Felipe was loved by Carolina, like I was loved by my Cosme. Fernanda loved Valentim, Cristiano, Christian, Álvaro, Ulisses, Eduardo and Dimitri, all for the first and only time. Cristiane loved Leandro, Priscilla loved Felipe, Raquel loved Leandro, Manoela loved Gustavo, Aline loved Maikon, Mariana loved Marcelo, Pedro loved Flávio like I love my Cosme. Natasha loved Igor, Iris loved Felipe, Lucas loved Gustavo, Ana loved Carlos and Guilherme loved Camila. Maísa was loved by André, Diana was loved by Kleber, Jefferson was the first love of Isadora, Lucas was the first love of Fernanda, Caio was Mariana's first, Maria Barbara was Diogo's first. I love my Cosme like Amanda loved Michael and Gisele loved Jean, like Suzane loved Rodrigo and like Flávia loved Rodrigo, like Chiara, Laia and Li Xin were loved by the same Gregório, like Williams loved Natália, like Francesca loved Massimiliano. Liliane loved Manuel, Catarina loved Eduardo and Achilles's first love was Suzane. I love my Cosme. Paola loved Anna, Mariana loved Rafael, Juliana loved Pedro, Tatiana loved Gabriel. I love my Cosme. Eduarda's first love was José, and Bárbara's Flavinho. I love my Cosme. Jéssica loved Mariana, Luana loved Tiago, Mariana loved Clarissa, Carolina loved Gustavo. I love my Cosme. Andrea loved Sérgio, Ingrid loved Jonathan, Daniela loved Maurício, Lola loved Elisa. I love my Cosme. Luciane was loved by Rafael, Felipe was loved by Luana like I was loved by my Cosme. Arthur loved Andréia, Lorena loved

Antônio Carlos, Laíza loved Vitor, Petra loved Thomas, Zeone loved Rafaela, Christina loved Jairo, Fábio loved André like I love my Cosme. Juliana loved Caio, Ana loved Álvaro, Daniela loved Jorge, Hellen loved Lilian. I love my Cosme. Patrícia loved José, Danielle loved João Pedro, Tatiane loved Marcos, Márcia loved Gilberto, Lisa loved Carlos Eduardo, Ronaldo loved Ângela, Kazue loved Renato, Márcia loved Cynthia like I love my Cosme. Ana loved Rafael, Paula loved Márcio, Tânia loved Fernando, Tatiana loved Gladson. Priscila loved Wilken, Bianca loved Bernardo, Sheyla loved Agostinho, Lucila loved Cadu, Alberto loved Marta. Messias loved Beatriz, Natália loved Gabriel, Cecília loved Gustavo. I love my Cosme. Like Beatriz loved Lorenzo, I loved my Cosme. Like Luciana loved Roberto, I love my Cosme. Gilberto loved Eda Lúcia, Luciana loved Roberto, Marcelo loved Luciana, Letícia loved Wanderley, Mayara loved Guilherme. I love my Cosme. Tatiana loved Alberto. Douglas loved Bruna, José loved Maraísa, Renata loved Bruno. I love my Cosme. Daniel loved Leilane, Ricardo loved Gabriel, Carla loved Silvana, Camila loved Mateus, Francisco loved Mariane, Rúbia loved Estêvão. I loved my Cosme. Luís loved Nayanne, Thiago loved Luciano, Fernanda loved Julia, Marcos loved Beatriz. Vanderson loved Júlio César. I loved my Cosme. Like Orlando loved Ana and Marta loved Fernando, like Caco loved Bia and Daniel loved Fernanda, Rodrigo loved Douglas and I loved my Cosme. Renato loved Débora, Suzana loved Frederico, Amanda loved Hudson, María loved Jorge, Ethel loved Décio, Rachel loved Petrônio. Like Ana loved Rafael and Ana was loved by Marina, like Afonso loved Tiago and Márcia, Luciano, Hugo loved Jonny and I loved my Cosme. Daniel loved Maria, Ricardo loved Karina, Abyellyes loved Poliana and Alessandra loved David. Like Anna loved André and Ana loved Carlos, I love my Cosme. Like Alice loved Quequi, like Bárbara loved Henrique, like Lídia loved Gabriel, like Marina loved Rafael, like Lívia loved Francisco, like Karina loved Ricardo, like Cassiano was loved by André, like Eduardo was loved by Samara, I love my Cosme. Like André loved Luca, like Tayana loved Nanda, I love my Cosme, my first and only.

36

The owner of the Flower of Queím bakery is Senhor Xande, Alexandre Matias, nicknamed "the Russki" or "the Portuguese," as happens with any white guy. (Around here they say "I'm going to the Portuguese," never "I'm going to the Flower.") He's the grandson of a Russian baker and the son of the goddess Iansã, he tells me. Fat, doughy and freckled, nose swollen and red from drink. Hair disheveled, gray, the nail of his left little finger very long—to pick his nose. He seems the complete man, one of those they no longer make, full of the demons that stir in Russian blood. He's so immense that the eye is always drawn to him first, no matter who's next to him.

He was standing in the doorway of the bakery, oblivious to everything like the father of the world: swaying in gray tracksuit bottoms, a burgundy shirt and hair a mess from torments, even early in the morning. The fragrance of warm bread ("The best bread rolls in the region," it says on the sign). In the corner, a bundle of offerings: clay pots with *farofa*, dried-up chicken legs, red candles, playing cards, seven of diamonds, seven of spades, seven of clubs. Between the *macumba* and the Portuguese, Renato was waiting for me.

Black T-shirt with COMPANY stamped on it, the letters catching fire, bleached jeans, clothes of a rich kid from the 1990s, probably secondhand. Cap with the brim bent into a ∩ and, on the front: GODIM FOR COUNCILLOR 18,926. Deodorant too strong for a boy with no armpit hair.

When he saw me, he cracked a smile. He held out his hand, I squeezed it, but from the sway of his body I understood he wanted to give me a hug. He wanted to go to the circus, the Garcia Circus was passing through Queím, let's go let's go? I explained that I couldn't, that I'm an old man, a cripple, I no longer have the energy. There comes an age when you can no longer be respectable in public. But look, he could come to the flat and watch TV.

HIM: We've got TV at home …

But he came anyway.

I bought bread, warm from the oven, finely sliced mortadella, artisanal butter (Flower of Queím brand, it comes in a can) and Coke. He's eating now, with his back to me, watching the TV. On the educational channel, a documentary about climate change. A desert engulfing Mexico and a large part of the USA.

"… 1,103 species will be extinct by two thousand and …"

He's hot. He just took off his shirt. A polar bear on TV, he points at the bear and smiles at me. He's very skinny. He has the same skin color that Cosme had, the same fig-colored nipples.

I ask and he says he's never been to the zoo.

37

ME: You know I knew your grandmother?

RENATO: (!)

He didn't take his eyes from the TV, but I saw his shoulders twitch in surprise.

ME: Your mother's mother. She worked at our house when I was your age.

RENATINHO: (Back still turned) No way.

ME: I knew your mother too, but she was younger than me. Do you remember? Your grandmother, she brought you up until ... (*Pause*) Your grandfather, I knew your grandfather too. He liked to go to the movies.

HIM: Me too. I've been millions of times.

ME: She was a simple person, your grandmother. A bit coarse, even. I can't tell you much about her, there's no point.

HIM: Mmm ...?

TV: ... arctic winds batter the earth ...

(*Pause*)

ME: Do you know who you look like most?

HIM: Who?

ME: Your grandfather. Your mother's father. He was always sucking cinnamon sticks. (*He babas*) It's true. Like a cigar. Hey. Look at me.

HIM: (*Still glued to the TV*) What?

ME: Do you know how to read yet?

HIM: Course. For years.

ME: I'm writing down our conversation. Later on I'll put who said what, how each of us spoke.

HIM: Why? Irreversible collapse.

TV: ... ecosystems will begin an irreversible collapse ...

ME: How many times have you seen this program?

HIM: Twice. The other time I came here it was on too, remember?

That's strange.

HIM: Twice. Mount Ki-ji-man ...

TV: ... Mount Kilimanjaro no longer has perpetual snow ...

ME: Hey. (*Pause*) Look at me.

38

What I see now is this: on the right-hand wall, my books locked in the china cabinet, piled up. I can see the worm-eaten cover of *The Jew's Revenge*. I've never read it. The cabinet has a mirror at the back, which hasn't seen the light for years (anyway, it's tarnished with rust). Beside the china cabinet, Renato, bare-chested, watches a documentary about Brazil's defeat in the 1950 World Cup. The movement on the screen hypnotizes him, his shoulders follow the runs of the players as though pulled by weak magnets. In the old footage, the players run much faster, as though they were all Buster Keaton.

ME: Don't you know we lost this one?

He doesn't hear.

Through the window, a cloud of beige dust obscures the apartment building in front. The cloud doesn't move. It's hot, but I can't remember the last time I felt sweaty. I sweat very little. My white T-shirts have never had yellow stains at the armpits. Three in the afternoon. Who will be this boy's first love?

He doesn't even like girls yet, let alone boys. But one day he will. The first love is the only one. The years, the sex and the small constructions (child, own home, savings) make us accept more easily the faded copies we say we love during our lives, but even our open graves, waiting for us, speak of its absence. The first love can only be the first love because there's a second, obviously. (On TV, goal for Uruguay. The boy cheers. He doesn't know who's who. It's all in black and white.) That open mouth of earth, salivating cold rain. Mine will try to shout my Cosme's name when they feed it my coffin. It will gag, but a grave doesn't choke.

In the paper the other day I read an interview with an artist, now an old man, who said he'd only gone to bed with women who looked alike: short blondes with some kind of mouth defect (cleft lip, various types of scar, the sequelae of a stroke). And he showed photos of his three ex-lovers and compared them to his current wife, who was photographed sitting by his side, with that tight-lipped smile. They were all alike, with a disfigured mouth, and identical to this artist's childhood sweetheart. I thought it was in bad taste, publishing it like that, with a photo and in Tuesday's paper, but I understood the impulse.

A.G.: *It's an attempt, then, to relive the first …*

B.C.O.: It's not just that. With identical faces, I can concentrate more on other things, because the background scenery is familiar …

39

RENATINHO: (*Still glued to the TV*) A kid's disappeared.

ME: What do you mean, disappeared?

RENATINHO: Disappeared, poof …

On TV, a documentary about Indians.

ME: Who?

HIM: From Rua do Almirante. They put photos on the lampposts. They were at the shopping mall asking if anyone had seen him.

ME: How long ago was this?

HIM: Dunno. I played soccer with him. Five times.

TV: … Indians in Brazil: who are they?

ME: Probably ran away from home.

HIM: No. (*Pause*) There was one that ran away, but this one…

He let his hand go floppy to say this one was queer.

ME: Did his father kick him out of the house?

He doesn't know.

ME: Did he go and live with his boyfriend?

HIM: Think so.

ME: Older boyfriend?

He doesn't know.

(And if I were to take a taxi that left me at the entrance to the mall? The doors would open automatically, the breath of the air-conditioning would invite me in. And if I were to go in, to see how the shoppers are reacting to the boy's disappearance? The granite floor would reflect the fluorescent lights, as if coated in plastic film. Neon. The same signs they have everywhere, the same smells as any food court, in malls from fancy Leblon to scruffy Costa Barros.

The high ceiling would echo the footsteps and laughter and conversations. So many people disappear in a city like Rio de Janeiro every year. Who cares …? This girl going up the escalator, in lilac leggings: she doesn't care. The proudly single forty-something mooning over shoes in the shop window doesn't care. The father trying the free sample of aftershave with his son doesn't care. The son, as soon as he starts middle school, will no longer care either, not about children that disappear, not about the Amazon, not about the ozone layer, not about anything. Only the elementary school teachers have the heart to care about these things, because they have to teach them in their classes. They generally use cardboard posters.)

40

I went to bed early. "You can stay there as long as you want," I said to the boy, who made an uh-hum noise without taking his eyes from the TV screen (the documentary about the Indians still on). I changed the channel, he didn't complain. A film, which I recognized after a few seconds: it was *The Bridges of Königsberg*. This is a classic, I said. At the end, this old man in the hat throws himself off the bridge. The father of this boy.

HIM: What for?
I didn't have the courage.
HIM: To swim in the river?
HIM: Did the boy jump too?

I changed the channel back to the documentary on the Indians.

I woke up feeling ill. I must have a fever.

I dreamed I was walking through the cemetery in Queím, which was in ruins, overrun by plants, the roots strangling the gravestones. I was looking for Maria Aína's grave; in the dream, only she knew where Cosme's body was. I couldn't find it because a lot of people had died on top of the old woman, who had disappeared under so many new graves and earth and rotten fruit. There are a lot of papaya trees in the cemetery here. Who eats these papayas? In the dream, I was thinking in the language of the cemeteries, the redundant language: from dust to dust, rest in peace, return from whence you came.

It's funny, because I know exactly where Cosme is buried.

In the middle of the night, Renato left. I think he came to say goodbye, I think I saw him standing beside the bed, half smiling. I shouldn't be sad, was what he said. I asked if it wasn't dangerous for him to go out so late and he said the sun was coming up. Then he put his right hand on my forehead and I felt how soft and warm it was. I don't know why he did it, I don't think he did either.

41

The egg room had a weird smell now. Since Mama had moved in there, she only left to go to the bathroom or have a shower. She'd polish her fake gold ornaments and look and polish and look and drink red wine and sleep and polish and look hard. Nothing was ever polished enough.

It was the beginning of her black phase, stained with sickly gold. There were no windows in the room. Paulina, already swollen with the baby, brought food, tried to tidy the piles of clothes, beat the sheets, give the corpus cavernosum an airing. From time to time I'd come to give her a hello or a kiss and I'd notice the smell. It wasn't a stink, because my mother didn't stink—she never went without rose-milk deodorant or French-Brazilian perfume, contraband from the street hawkers in Cidade Nova. It was the smell of a bathroom that's been disinfected, but locked shut for hours. The smell of teeth almost rotten, but recently brushed.

(She and Dad traded words, yes, I remember. They traded them, but didn't trade them back. One of them was stuck with the other's words and that was that. Conversation didn't exist, only monologue existed. They didn't kiss. I never saw the two of them hold hands again.)

Dad worked shifts and drank in his free time. Drunk, he was a slick-as-Vaseline best pal. He talked and talked and said he loved us with those slippery lips. One day, he insisted he was going to build a tree house for us, chose an almond tree on the street and gave it a few slaps on the trunk to see if it would hold. It would! The next day, he got planks, ropes and nails. On the third day, he sobered up. The planks were stolen before the dew could rot them.

Sometimes Dad would sink into a silence and everybody saw on his face that he was in pain, everybody thought it was because he'd seen so many people die.

42

We were sitting on the sofa, me and Cosme, my crutches crossed, two bars lying between my legs. Our family had a sofa in the house like everybody else. Three seats, scratchy material, a soft lead color, paid for in installments, a respectable Brazilian family sofa. I must have been quiet for several minutes, because Cosme asked me what was wrong.

"Are you sad?"

"No."

"Is it because the old woman died? (*Pause*) Is it because of your ma?"

I said no and no and went back to being quiet.

I was doing calculations.

I think it was around then that I began to like calculating and cataloging and classifying things. I know very well who I am today, that I have a clinical eye, I mean to say. But I don't know when it began. It came from before, it was before the death of Cosme. After he was murdered, I could have become someone who really loved baby photos, a professional victim, a religious nut, a halfwit, a nervous wreck, but no. I'm this person here. (Ex.: A human being cries 121 liters of tears, on average, during their life. The heart beats 35 million times per year.)

I was calculating: how many liters of semen had I produced up to that moment? Less than half a jam jar? More than a shot of cachaça? Knots already drank cachaça, but we couldn't, no sir. We weren't men yet, no sir. How much cum does the average man produce in his life? A ten-liter flask, a soft-drink bottle? The obsession that boys have for these things ... My Cosme put his hand on my shoulder, then briefly ran his fingers through my hair.

"Don't be sad."

Then he tried to curl back into my arms, like he'd seen me do on the day Dad cried because they killed his friend, but the crutches made the maneuver difficult. I tried to take the two bars out of the way, but there wasn't time: he soon became shy and pulled away. He smiled, hehhehed and repeated:

"Don't be sad."

43

I saw my mother naked once. She was getting out of the shower, without a towel or anything, still dripping. She was rushing back to her cave, missing her golden eggs. And I saw her flab swinging, despite her thinness. The sagging flesh of my withered mother, a woman elongated like the duchesses of England and slightly mad like the queens of Portugal. She had the breasts of a chubby boy, which won't become real breasts because they can't. The belly of a woman twice a mother hung wrinkled, without a single hair. She was the age I am today, more or less. The buttocks of a smoker, skull-like, jiggled; one, two, four steps and Mama saw me and almost tripped as she disappeared into her room. From inside came a stifled oh, and she slammed the door.

I'd never seen a naked woman. It was like seeing a painting by one of these modern artists, what's the name of that painter again? I don't know, I'm not going to try to find out. It's ugly, but it's pretty, like that, from a distance. All those decrepit details. Varicose veins, bald spots, shriveled patches, discolorations.

After that she didn't look me in the face for a week. She only spoke to me through a crack in the door. "Mama has the flu, son." She didn't want to contaminate me.

44

I keep thinking about the boy who disappeared, who played soccer here in these streets to which the tarmac doesn't stick properly (tarmac doesn't last as long in the heat, it blisters and bursts into holes), between the 1970s vans, the tail-finned

Monzas, the Ford Belinas, the Volkswagen Brasílias, the whole junkyard the beach neighborhoods no longer wanted.

Where did the kid go? To Copacabana and Ipanema, where the actresses and the money are? Sun. To Humaitá, where the sea still echoes and the wretched try to live alongside the cars and the restaurants and the jugglers at the traffic lights. Or downtown, close to Candelária, where at night passersby relieve their stress by breaking curbstones on the heads of the street kids, scattering brains everywhere. ⁙ I've seen it all, because I've walked around these places. I've seen Christ the Redeemer up close. Where did that kid go? He's where the big shots analyze economic strategies and present them to the newspapers. Zero sacred kinship or understanding, not a hint of pity. Just the tired old hunger for carbon and calcium, flesh and fang.

He must have been arrested, the kid.

People disappear easily.

45

Not even two weeks had passed since Maria Aína's funeral when Paulina decided to make ox tongue for lunch, just like the old woman had taught her. In the center of the table, the oval glass dish, a muddy slime at the bottom, a brownish fat that, when cooled, would turn to gelatin. Five, seven, eleven slices of tongue. I thought it was weird at the time and I still do. The old woman was hardly cold in her grave, and the smell of that warm meat filled the house.

My father, head of the table, licked his lips and made an mmmmm to please the cook. Me on the right, my Cosme on the left, "Sit, Paulina," my father said, and she sat next to me.

Without ceremony. My mother, locked in the egg room, I don't know what she was going to have for lunch, but I remember at the time she was crazy for sunflower seeds. She ate them like a rat, and the shells carpeted the floor.

I heard it, I did. No one can say I didn't hear the tongue muttering on the plate. Though obviously I didn't understand what it said. Dead ox. Ox or cow?

Paulina's skin had the smell of dry sweat and coconut soap. Her intestines probably had it too. I don't know what my father saw in her to keep looking and smiling, staring and smiling. First, he asked some medical questions: how she was feeling with the baby, if she was bleeding in such and such a way, if she was feeling such and such a nausea, if it hurt there … She smiled awkwardly and answered "Goodness, Senhor Cruz!" when my father asked a question about her hairy parts. He laughed.

"And your husband?"

"Not my husband, no, sir."

"Good …"

"Should be, though."

"What does he do?"

"Works on a building site."

(The killer had the smell of dry sweat and cement dust, then, beneath the sickening perfume of the cinnamon.)

My father ate. (I ate too. We all did.) Then he excused himself and got up before everyone else. He came up behind me and ran his hand across my head. I saw my dad's smile reflected in Cosme's, who returned any smile he was given, no matter who from. The hand, still suspended, was lifted to the back of Paulina's neck, she shivered all over, oh, Senhor Cruz. They hahahaed.

I was furious.

We spent a lot of time at the old slave house. Maybe too much. There was one day, we were talking, sitting on the ground, in a circle. A few blades of sunlight poked through the humid forest, green half-light, buzzing noises. That's when they showed me the version of the kid's song "Run, agouti" they'd made up.

Run, agouti	Run, agouti
in the house of your auntie.	I screwed your auntie.
Run, green ivy	Run, green ivy
in the house of your granny.	I wouldn't screw your granny.
Hankie in your hand	Dick in your hand
falls on the sand,	shits on the sand,
pretty little girl,	pretty little girl,
my sweetheart.	my sweetheart.

The circle of boys moved, torsos puffing, arms in the air or hands clapping, asses rubbing the ground in search of catharsis. "Run, agouti …" the singing continued, getting louder. One got up and ran around us, behind us, imitating the original game. Furtive strokes on the ears and taps on the backs of necks. Curse words, belly laughs. I couldn't laugh; I cracked the sad smile of my sister when she helped me be less crippled: eyebrows arched in a sad solemnity. Little Camilo doesn't see the humor in eff-all, stop being a dick, "pretty little girl, my sweetheart." They had other versions of songs in a circle and versions of the same "Run, agouti" (I screwed your auntie, I shat in your sink-y, I licked your little thingy, let me stick it in please, I killed your pony …).

They started again. "Run, agouti …"

How tedious, people. The artists on TV, in the sci-fi films and mystery dramas, the little Napoleons, the bridge jumpers and the sad poets ... They're all just the negatives of the same tedium, the other side of a coin that was always dull, stick it up your ass! the life of one person is exactly like the life of another, all that changes is the address. And there aren't that many elements in the universe, all of them classifiable. From a shell to the shelling of Gaza there's not much difference. Listen to this, ocean and explosion both sound like waves. Between a man and a rat, there are only three hundred genes of difference. I remember reading one day: an army of monkeys typing randomly on typewriters will end up writing a Shakespeare play. We jacked off a lot in that forest. The boys always wanted to go to my house to swim in the pool but were too embarrassed to ask.

47

I haven't seen Renato for almost two weeks. I'm starting to worry. I go to the bakery in the morning and the afternoon, and the boy hasn't been there for eleven days. I mean, I thought he'd come here to the flat every day, that he'd always be waiting for me, a natural kind of thing, a meet-me-on-the-corner romance. I don't know where he lives or who the woman that takes care of him is. (Though it wouldn't be hard to find out.) Senhor Xande at the bakery doesn't know where he is, he hasn't seen him. Whenever I ask, I look deep into his Russian face, inspect his plucked-chicken skin, the red veins of an alcoholic, the smell of flour. His eyes are swimming-pool green. "The boy has no one," he said. He understood my worry. "We get attached to these creatures and then we suffer."

The Russki has a scar right under his left eye. He almost went blind. A shot from a bean gun, he told me, a kid's gun, made with clothespins, a matchbox with two AA batteries inside and the inner tube of a tire. They hit him in the face with a bean and ran away. They weren't from here in Queím, the kids. Children. He laughed in his crabby way when he told the story. These streets are a Wild West for kids.

He hiked up his pant leg, nearly falling headfirst, and showed me another wound, a gaping red hole at knee height, the edges ugly with pus. A little lower, on the shin, the scar of a similar wound, equally badly treated. These were from slingshots, builder's gravel, a few gray stones with little black spots, the size of plums. The kids around here did it, he explained, but he couldn't identify whose kids they were.

Only then did I discover that the Russki is a constant target of attacks, a fat dog hated for no reason. The slightest move brings a pack of them howling past the bakery and then come the stones, bits of wood, fruit, whatever they can get their hands on. Once they smashed the glass display case.

And this is the man who makes everyone's bread.

"Not your boy," he said. "He actually defends me."

48

From the apartment next door, Grumá's place, comes a muffled samba. I can barely hear it, but I know it's that Nelson Cavaquinho record that starts with "Last Judgment": "I want to have eyes to see … the evil disappear." The sun shall shine once again and so on. He always listens to the same record, sometimes he sings along, noisily out of tune, but he hasn't even said hello to me for over a month. I don't like music much, but I like this one by Nelson. I always listen to it. It's the only record I have. It was Grumá who recommended it to me.

He isn't singing today.

"There's a boy here for you," the building manager told me over the intercom. "At my place." I went downstairs as fast as I could, the door to 102 was ajar, Renato sitting on the couch, belly sticking out, chin lowered, as though awaiting punishment. When he saw me, he gave a triumphant smile, got up and went to leave. The building manager stopped him with a hand on the shoulder.

The kid had been trespassing in the building, was what he said. A genuine resident came in, he took advantage of the gap and slipped in at the same time. "Lucky the doorman grabbed him, if not, what would he have done? These street kids... can't be allowed, it looks bad for me, it looks bad for the building. (*Pause*) I couldn't believe it when he mentioned your name. You've never caused any problems, a model member of the community. You have this symmetrical face despite the ... well, a face of good character, do you know the phrenologist Lombroso? (*He tries to feel my face; I refuse.*) Do you know this child? He smells nice, but I'm no fool. Sometimes they don't do anything wrong, but who'd put their hand in the fire for them? Would you? Put your hand in the fire?" I gave the boy my hand. "I know him," and we left without another word. The building manager stared after us like a police dog that had fallen from the van.

The building manager—whose name is José Clay—is a clear T. de M. Jr. ♂ type. (Or he's something deeper. Perhaps, under the skeleton of personality and the fat layer of habit, we all have the soul of a building manager.)

I'd had no news for twenty-three days. In that time, Grumá left another envelope with ninety reais in my mailbox (is he avoiding me? Because?); I had the flu and got over the flu; the Russki from the bakery took a few more stonings (but they didn't break any glass). Where was the boy? No one could imagine the horrors I imagined. I could barely manage to get through my daily routine. And where had he been?

"Around ..."

"I thought you'd disappeared."

He hahahaed.

50

ME: Do you have any friends?

RENATINHO: I've got Manuca and I've got Tiziu.

For a moment, I thought it was the same Tiziu I knew when I was a kid, but obviously it wasn't. It's a nickname that spans generations. The population of Tizius in Queím is always around half a dozen individuals, regardless of the decade. The bird itself, which inspired the name, I've never seen. It's blue-black and sings "ti-ziu, ti-ziu" (I heard a recording online), that's all: "ti-ziu, ti-ziu" its entire life. When a black character becomes famous on TV, the number of Tizius tends to decrease, because the kids have other nicknames to use: Uncle Macalé the comedian, Mussum the actor, Pelé, Vera Verão the drag queen, Obama.

ME: And what do you do with them?

RENATINHO: Uh, everything.

ME: And is it fun?

RENATINHO: Um, yeah.

He turned on the TV. A documentary about marine life. After a few minutes staring at the aquarium, he asked if I took the bus.

ME: Sometimes. Do you?

RENATINHO: I've taken it eighty-two times.

ME: This year?

RENATINHO: No, ever.

He wanted to know if I feel sad when people don't sit next to me on the bus, because I do, he said, and gulped down the rest of the sentence and turned it into another story about how he once saw a really ugly man, whose mouth was stitched up with scars, on the 367 (Queím–Praça XV). The bus was full and no one sat next to him. He didn't stink, no. Not even the smell of sweat. He described lots of details: his clothes, his five-o'clock shadow, the shape and color of his shoes, his tie; but what I remember most, the boy said, was how the man leaned his head against the window glass and closed his eyes because he was sad.

51

It was in broad daylight. On the corner outside the house. I remember the sun on my forehead, on my scalp, ⁚⁚ on my arms, the sweat on my skin, sticking to my crutches. The eternal haze of beige dust. My first kiss.

We were walking along, and we stopped at this spot in the photo, which is four blocks from here. The conversation wasn't about anything important. Stopping was a bit awkward, because we had no reason to suddenly not keep walking. It was my Cosme who stopped first, I planted my crutches and steadied myself, with a face like a silly question. Silence. Then he gave me a kiss. He grabbed my two arms and tugged (gently, so as not to knock me down), and I went, Bettishly, Davishly. His lips were dry, the splinters of hard skin pricked me. I passed my tongue over them to soften them. Salty taste. He opened his mouth, tongue on tongue like the ox tongue Maria Aína used to make. After the grossness of the bolus, it was as though we'd had this desire forever.

I would never feel safe again. I discovered it right then. My heart started to cough freezing air into my veins. Childish really, panicking over a first kiss. Later, when we start to pay our own bills, we feel the same thing. A helplessness. During our first serious illness, helplessness. On our important birthdays every ten years, especially the first, helplessness. Then you get used to it. Nowadays, I go to the bakery, helpless, I buy bread, helpless, processed ham, helpless, cheese, which is more expensive, only every now and again.

(It's unlikely the killer was nearby at the time. But in my memory this scene almost has the faint smell of cinnamon.)

52

The next day, it rained. It was a Monday, and it was August. The sky dawned clear and then it heated up, heated up so much that, around nine, it rained. I couldn't remember the last time it had rained. (I also don't remember how long it's been since it rained these days. The air's always humid, but it doesn't rain. The sky, swimming-pool blue, just threatens to.) It was a single downpour, enough to refresh the plants and rinse the dead cockroaches back into the drains.

Then the sun came out again. ⸱⸱⸱ And an idyll began, the only one I've ever experienced.

At seven, Paulina came to call me for school and I pretended to be sick, the flu, a cough. I groaned. She smiled and said I really must be, because Senhor Cosme was also poorly, that's how she said it: "Senhor Cosme," "poorly." She thought we'd planned it, but we hadn't. She consulted my father and he agreed. That we should stay at home; a boy has to skip class from time to time. A sign we were more and more like brothers. Good comrades, that's what they thought. Child comrades.

After the rain, Cosme came to my room and squeezed into my bed. The heat wasn't as bad anymore. His tongue was rough and warm, like his hands. The idyll would end in exactly fourteen days.

Every idyll ends in a storm, and from storm to flood only takes a couple of hours. Everyone knows how terrible our sewage system is, the underground pipes and tunnels, mayors come, mayors go ... The flood soon becomes a deluge, and the deluge, an ocean. And then the mourning begins, which is slow and quiet on the surface of the water, but fertile in the depths: the plankton soon appears, corals form, fish and algae and octopuses and schools of dolphins are born and whales spit water upward and at some point the bereaved revive. I stayed. My Cosme disappeared and I stayed, like an amputated octopus tentacle, which stays alive even after it's cut off, and roams around looking for food. When it finds some, it takes the food and makes the gesture of bringing it to its mouth, as if it were still connected to the body. I learned that in the documentary on marine life I watched with Renatinho.

Even now I'm living out the grief of the octopus, or in fact the grief of a piece of the octopus, a ridiculous piece, because octopus tentacles regenerate, just like a lizard's tail.

53

On Tuesday, there was no escape: school (him to one, me to another). He waited for me as we were leaving, a present in his hands. It was a lead plane wrapped in pink paper and bakery string: a model Spitfire Mk I PR, type A, which caused no damage, only went on reconnaissance flights.

I asked where he got it and he said, hawhawing, that he stole it from Iguatemi. From Iguatemi's house, from his bedroom.

Shithead Iguatemi. Poorer than me Iguatemi. Iguatemi who would never be a sailor. He could die by drowning. I died of jealousy.

Before he died, my Cosme gave me so many things …:

2 cloudy pebbles (the rarest ones);

14 black pebbles;

1 vinyl record found in a dumpster (Victor Talking Machine Company, with the little dog staring into the gramophone);

4 models representing Indian tribes;

1 box of Guarany matches;

3 shoes, singular (2 women's, 1 men's);

1 white brooch;

1 porcelain owl missing an ear;

12 assorted clothing buttons;

1 brown beret;

1 book by Darcy Ribeiro without the cover;

2 women's blouses (pink and blue);

1 copy of *Seventh Heaven* celebrity gossip magazine with Tarcísio Meira's face on the cover ('Regina Duarte reveals the ending of *Fire Upon The Earth*');

1 can of butter biscuits (I kept the can);

1 red lotus flower (it was pressed inside the magazine);

2 black stamp pads;

1 cream bun (I kept the napkin, which lost its grease stains years ago);

1 pin with a red tip;

3 blank cassette tapes (they're still blank).

At the gates to my school (his was a state school), I said I didn't want to see my classmates. Smiling, he understood; he wasn't afraid. "What do you want, then?" and I wanted him to suck me while I was still soft, I wanted my dick to harden inside his mouth. I said this and the only reason I don't regret it to this day was because he replied "OK then," with no shock whatsoever, no insults or giggles. But in the end it never happened. That day, we simply forgot. The twelve after that too.

(I kept everything he gave me, along with documents and other junk. It's in a wood and leather trunk, inherited from my mama.)

54

The boy wanted mortadella, Renato, and fresh bread. (He's here all the time, now. He comes straight from school, when he goes. I don't force him. The woman who takes care of him hasn't even tried to find out where he is. There's no photo of the boy on the lamp posts nor a search party at the mall.) I went to the bakery and when I got back, he was watching a plume of smoke rise on the TV screen. Today is August 13, 2014. It's 9:24 p.m. and the jet assigned to Eduardo Campos, candidate for president of the Republic, has crashed in Santos.

RENATINHO: That's in Santos. Santos is on São Paulo beach.

ME: What is it?

RENATINHO: A helicopter crashed.

I made his snack. He ate, drinking Coke to soften the bread-butter-mortadella, while they updated the news. (In the apartment next door, Grumá was listening to the Nelson Cavaquinho record: "This world is a school ... don't forget to learn, my love ...") It wasn't just a helicopter, it was a plane that crashed into a helicopter. The air force confirms one story, disconfirms the other. Or perhaps it was the presidential candidate's plane after all, turns out there wasn't a helicopter, just a plane. It crashed into a residential neighborhood, destroyed a gym and a lady's house. Anyone else's house? The reporters don't know. Seems like it was the presidential candidate's plane. It was, confirms a congressman from the same party, who says he's a personal friend. We had lunch (rice and chicken nuggets with potato chips; I don't know how to cook beans). I ate a lot. But why did it crash? Experts are called in to give their opinion. The search begins. Soon, everyone will make a statement. The common people cry in interviews. One of them says they salvaged the candidate's head, they saw the candidate's blue eyes. I don't know, I think it's important to mention it. A plane crashed, the plane was small. What at the start of the morning was smoke became, by lunchtime, a candidate for the presidency of Brazil.

RENATINHO: I've never been in a helicopter. Not even a plane.

ME: Do you want to someday?

He nodded yes and burped Coke.

55

Wednesday. Outside, the carpet of the pavement unfurled for us, Cosme and me, walking side by side. Ahead, an altar awaited, one formed entirely of kids, some sitting, some leaning against the facade of the old slave house, Knots smoking from a hole that had once been a window. My groom tried to give me his hand, but mine were tied up with walking, crutches, my school uniform, my skin stinking of the rancid morning—math and Portuguese classes, a surprise geography test. I'd bombed.

The sun at its peak, though it wasn't very hot. ⁛ Cosme was more confident than me. He knew exactly what to do. I just guessed. He was wearing his uniform too, walking slowly alongside me, a kind of waltz, as though dressed in a tailcoat, with a gold tie and shiny new shoes, his chest puffed out. He waved from a distance, and they waved back. (Where was the killer just then?) He'd had a test that morning too, in history. Cosme was good at history. He never found out his grade. (I didn't either. The principal gave his report card to my father, but the teachers hadn't put the marks. Only those from the first term.)

My face isn't ugly. I've got a few Roman features, soft and slightly plump from good living, with full lips on a smallish mouth, a little nose that looks straight, but up close isn't quite. I've always visited the dentist regularly. Curved eyebrows and curly hair, today almost entirely gray. My skin, marble white with green veins, is no longer smooth. I was a good-looking child. We were a good-looking family. Cosme's and my kid would have looked like an Egyptian god.

We arrived at the boys' feet (there were no girls). He squeezed my hands with his, leaned in, and gave me a you-may-kiss-the-bride kiss.

For a long time they didn't react, their faces frozen as if they'd seen a man with the black head of a dog. I imagined, in panic, one of them jumping up and kicking my left knee, breaking my crippled leg; another punching Cosme on the nose, forcing his mouth open and grinding his teeth against the rough wall. I imagined them grabbing us and pouring boiling oil on our skin. That they'd drive a steel bar into our thighs, sealing us together like a plastic toy. That they'd get up without saying a word, such was their disappointment, and walk away in disgust. Or they'd try to argue with us, out of friendship: but if everybody was like you, humanity would no longer reproduce! Or they'd laugh, hahaha, heheha, hawhawha. I imagined all that old stew of horrors, in which they put the severed heads and flesh of queers burnt at the stake. An old stew, reheated and reseasoned with each fresh generation of boys, ever since the first emperor of Rome thought that to be clean a man should remain a virgin, while doubly filthy was a man who lay with another man.

Their faces softened after the initial shock, they began to stir, and look at one another. They had an obligation of anger, disgust and mockery, but no one wanted to start. They stared at us. We didn't smile. We stared back.

Then Knots jumped from the window back onto the street, tossing his cigarette away (the embers sparked on the road). Hearts readied: this was it. My vision went dark around the edges, then grew darker until there were just two little holes left, a double-barreled shotgun. They'd shoot first, I hadn't seen enough cowboy films. The boys got to their feet, blood rushing to their legs, ready to pounce. I'm going to fall. Cosme held me, and I steadied myself on my crutches, I'm going to fall. Knots stepped forward.

He stopped in front of the gang. Smiled to make peace. Now I could see better, but my knees were trembling. The boys behind, oblivious to Knots's smile. (*Pause*) Iguatemi looked at Zetimó, and I saw it: Zetimó's arm picking up speed and becoming a punch that landed right on Iguatemi's neck. Zetimó looked bewildered, and Iguatemi fell coughing to the ground.

He gasped for air as though he'd just been saved from drowning, his hands tearing at his chest. Air.

Zetimó was staring at his arm, his arm and the boys, the boys and Iguatemi, who was now surrounded, my Cosme in the middle, on his knees. Porky put both hands on his fallen friend's chest and began to push, like he'd seen them do on TV. You're going to give him mouth-to-mouth? You'll finish him off, shit for brains! Then Tiziu gave him a get-out-of-it barge with his shoulder. Porky fell over.

Fat prick!

By now Iguatemi was half coughing, half laughing.

A pause and the boys advanced on Zetimó, hungry for revenge. Including my Cosme. Somebody stuck out a leg and Zetimó fell, not far from Iguatemi. One kick, two in the ribs. He took it, raised his hand to plead for a truce, nodded OK, OK. Knots slapped him on the ear, then Cosme gave Knots a shove, telling him it was enough.

They all eyeballed one another, weighing up the possibility of a mass brawl. Iguatemi sat up, breathing heavily. Zetimó stuck his fingers in his mouth to see if he'd lost any teeth. Stop, Porky said, for fuck's sake, stop!

57

Afterward, to have something to say, Knots commented that I was white and Cosme was brown, I was rich and he was poor. A gold digger. And then laughed, because you can't just change the subject and move on either.

And that was that.

In a few hours, they were over their beatings, and got used to the idea that their two friends were boyfriends. Only a bruise would remain and that was OK. When we kissed they'd say yuck, or every now and then they'd throw things: dirt, a bunch of weeds. They weren't ready to joke about it, but they stopped calling Cosme names and shoving him around. For two weeks, they respected us.

The next day or the day after, I forget, Tiziu's sister gave birth at home. Twins, a boy and a girl, with a mother but no father. Yuck, they said when they heard about the placenta, and threw bunches of weeds at him, and called him a shit-for-brains. They were probably more disgusted by his sister than by us. They still hadn't completely lost their fear of girls.

58

The news spread, but the scandal didn't come from the tender faces of my friends. It came from the faces of the old women and the well-brought-up young ladies—I'm certain it was the hard faces of the old women that were offended first. No doubt one of them was spying on the street, with the tsk-tsk-tsk cocked on her tongue, ready to fire at the slightest sign of indecency: an unaccompanied woman, savagery in the traffic, a *macumbeiro*, a drunk or pickpocket. But a kiss between boys she'd never seen. Perhaps she didn't even have time to click her tongue, no doubt she went straight to call the youngest young lady (wherever there are old women, there are young ladies). Come see, come see. And the come-see of one multiplied into ten, two hundred, three hundred did-you-sees? In the bread line or the afternoon house calls, did you see that boys are going around kissing now? In broad daylight, shamelessly, an indecency, two hundred indecencies! What's the world coming to.

None of this reached my father's ears. Of course. As far as I know, he died thinking it was women who didn't like me.

59

I try to remember, but the things my Cosme did and said in those last two weeks have been disappearing, the true memory is lost. The way I looked at him has also almost completely faded. Here today, tomorrow who knows: everything can be wiped out forever and I'll have nothing to cling to.

(You'll see this is the last revelation before oblivion.)

That's why I liked the customers at the antique shop. My antique shop in the Cartago Arcade, the famous Cartago. I've never had as much money as I had then. I even lived near the Praça do Lido for a while. But I ended up bankrupt all the same.

I took over the spot from an old man called Amílcar Meireles, and almost all the customers continued to call me Amílcar, even those who'd known me a long time. It was the name on the sign.

From the counter, you could just see the Our Lady of Copacabana Church. I could identify my clients from a long way
off. They stood out from the frenzy of the avenue, from the
brute force of Copacabana, a neighborhood that, even today
and even on Sundays, moves with the violence of an eternal
Friday-afternoon rush hour: car accidents, horns honking,
street brawls, infidelities, property speculation, catcalls, wolf
whistles, price hikes, falls on the hot tarmac. But the customers were oblivious to all this, Copacabana wasn't for them. I
recognized them from afar. They were the ones who knew,
even back then, that the hopes of a new bossa nova were over.

Good people. Housewives obsessed with knickknacks, collectors of 1960s brooches, of out-of-print books, of outdated
encyclopedias, of lilac umbrellas; collectors of newspapers and
magazines, of broken toys and electrical appliances and ridiculous shoes. The kind of people who think that nothing that
has existed should disappear. People willing to pay whatever it
takes. And even so I didn't make that much money.

People who later die. (A lot of people die in Copacabana.)
And these people don't usually have anyone who'd be inter-
ested in the junk they've accumulated. Enter the janitor, who
boxes everything up and throws it away. (It was a garbage company called Santa Eufêmia that collected this junk.) Every now
and then, on my way to the shop, I'd come across these cardboard boxes on top of the rubble from building work and ren-
ovations, and inside there was always something I could sell:
photo albums, records, books, clothes, hats. All for free, but if it
wasn't for me, these things would end up in a dump in the outer
suburbs. The Santa Eufêmia garbage company has no mercy.
(Eufêmia was martyred for praying when she shouldn't, and
nowadays she's given her name to a small asteroid, 630 Eufêmia,
which will never be on a collision course with the earth.)

When I die, I know someone will come in here (the janitor,
my sister, the building manager) and stuff everything that's

mine into a cardboard box, which will end up in one of those dumpsters (I don't know from which company). I hope someone finds it, because inside will be my notebooks, the photo of the singular boy, Cosme's report card, my childhood drawings ... My things have a memory, and their memory is tied to Cosme's, and his memory is tied to other people's, and so on. How I liked the shop's customers. They knew that, in the end, we're all connected; our bonds are cardboard boxes full of junk.

Dumpster, have mercy.

60

There was one of them, I don't remember his name now. A very white kid with gray hair. He only bought manuals: on trout fishing, on guns, on confectionery, on style and comportment, on Saint Cyprian magic, whatever. He once stopped to talk to me. He said he was studying for a master's and that everyone in the entire country was a police chief. "A nation of police chiefs," was what he said. The really smart ones were the judges. The really smart ones invented the laws. The really smart ones ordered the laws to be invented and no one knew who they were. But no one wanted to be them, he said.

These days everyone wants to be them. The race has evolved.

ME: What do you want to be when you grow up?

RENATINHO: Helicopter driver.

61

The sun opens cracks in the pavements, always. The local government tries to fix them, but the sun works against them, drying out the cement and reopening the gaps. The newspapers attack the council, but the sun yellows the pages. The citizens complain, but the sun anesthetizes their anger and offers them the beach. The sun hates everyone, without distinction. ⋰⋱ The other day a councillor tripped over one of those solar cracks and fell mouth-first onto the stairs of the government chambers. He almost died. He was already old, Your Lordship Councillor Chico Sforzinda (Popular Party), a staunch supporter of demolishing the favelas. He wore false teeth. It was in the papers.

We were sitting down. Cosme was yanking up the weeds that grew in the cracks in the pavement, as if they'd forced their way through the concrete. He didn't say anything. He barely looked at me. I asked what the problem was, he didn't answer. I thought he was beginning to stop loving me. Any little silence from him and I was already predicting the end, beginning to plan my suicide. I was afraid, then angry.

HIM: Who do you like best, your dad or your ma?"

"My mama."

I saw his head had jerked to the left. He grimaced, cramp in the belly, the embarrassing kind. Cosme knew my parents were on the verge of separating. And he would never stay with Mama. The sun intruded. ⋰⋱ I put out my hand, opening and closing it, asking for his:

"Help me."

He stood and pulled me up. I steadied myself on my crutches, still angry:

"And if I have to go away?"

"Go where?"

"Nova Iguaçu."

"Dunno where that is."

"New Delhi."

"Dunno where that is."

"You don't want to go?"

"Go where?"

Then he hugged me.
(Stupid Cosme. Ass. Understood nothing.)
I hugged him tighter too.

Today, the weeds still grow in the cracks in the cement. They find space, take root. The other day, the building manager sent around a note saying the tree in front needed to be chopped down, since the council does nothing. It's a huge fig tree, the roots have broken up the pavement. He asked for my contribution, my signature, money.

The tree has already strangled the curb and is now advancing toward the entrance gates. The roots have infiltrated the pipes, which explains the earthy taste of the tap water. Who planted it? Nobody remembers. The building manager said that if we don't take action an old person could die. Dona Vera from 701 has already tripped on the baked pavement. She could have broken her elbow!

I didn't contribute.

I think it's beautiful when trees do this. For years, the roots grow quietly under our feet, grow, harden, spread, straining against the surface of the pavement.

I wish my ear was sharp enough to hear the sound of the root wearing away at the cement, pushing, gaining space. The prolonged, muffled friction, the creaking of wood, the soft whistles in the dark, the miasmas. And one day, finally, the light.

I wish I could live for centuries, so the victory would seem as quick as a punch. I'd like to see the street sweepers picking up the debris after months of phone calls and other complaints, petitions, visits to the Secretary for Parks and Gardens. The authorities in this city barely move!

I wish I was the tree.

"Go where?" was what my Cosme asked.

Wherever there was space.

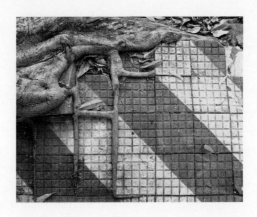

The boy tries to change the channel. The cable TV is down.

ME: There's no signal.

He doesn't hear. Squeezes with his thumb, the nail has a small white streak. The name of this is leukonychia, it's not a serious disease. In my day, they said that when these marks appeared it was because someone was in love with you.

They also said that, if you can imagine what a person will look like when they're old, it's because you love them. But you have to really be able to see them. You have to be moved by the decrepitude of your beloved.

ME: How long have you been here?

RENATINHO: Seventy-four days.

ME: How long do you think you'll stay?

(*Pause*)

ME: Can you imagine me when I was your age?

He gives a few chuckles of relief and says no, I'm way too old. I can, I say, I can imagine what he'll be like when he's old.

He laughs, but doesn't continue the conversation, just stares at the snowstorm on the TV, trembling all over. He's afraid of having to leave.

(The exact image I had of my Cosme is gone, I can't imagine what he'd be like old. While he was alive, I never thought about it.)

64

The killer came out of the movie theater. We were sitting on the pavement, Cosme and I holding hands, Iguatemi telling the story about the time a Brazilian ship attacked a school of dolphins thinking it was a German submarine ("Liar!" "It's true!" "Tell the truth, Iguatemi!" "It's true, my dad told me!"). It was a bloodbath. Then the killer walked past, like the other times—cinnamon stick in his mouth, smell of sweat and cement. He'd been to see a film on his lunch break, while the other builders slept in the sun. ːˌː How was he allowed to take such a long lunch break? I don't know whether he was the builders' boss. An engineer he was not.

(This I remember: at the Maier Cinema they were rerunning that John Wayne film *The Man Who Shot Liberty Valance*. Me and Cosme went to see it the next day. The usher was a friend of our gang and let us in the back. We sat in the last row. There was no popcorn. It was our only trip to the movies.) I've watched that film many times since: "Hey, pilgrim! When the legend becomes fact, print the legend." This here is the West.

The killer nodded and kept on walking. We nodded back. No one was afraid of him anymore. I don't know if he saw us holding hands. He must have seen. He wrinkled his nose and turned away, but he could have just been sniffing his own drunkard's stink. All the bricklayers drank black Xingu beer in the middle of the working day.

I'd like to say I lived two years in two weeks with my Cosme, but no. Two decades. These things don't happen. We lived fourteen days. I loved every inch of him, but not every minute. In all, there were 20,160 minutes, many lost to school and showers, to lunches. When we were together, still others were lost in silence, with the becauses of silence. Was it because of this or that, was it because I had to do my homework, was it because you don't like me anymore? We said we loved each other, but that wasn't the same thing it is today.

And fear, a fear that would only be healed if he and I became even more than conjoined twins, a single item. A thing. Two arms, two legs, hair, stink of boy, white-coffee skin, face of an Egyptian god, one penis, head of a dog. The monster that weighs men's hearts after they die.

Tuesday (on the following Monday, he'd be dead). It must have been around four in the afternoon, a time when the house became a ghost: the low sound of the pressure cooker, psst-psst, no pressure, psst-psst-psst, Paulina was making dinner, psst-psst-psst-psst. Dad sleeping for the overnight shift, Mama holed up with her golden eggs. Cosme was asleep on my side of the bed, the sheet smothering our recent heat. The hairs on his leg tickling me. The two of us, the ten-tentacled monster. A droplet of sweat on his forehead.

I heard heavy steps outside, feet in boots. My room always smelt strongly of wood, from all the wooden furniture. The door wasn't locked. The footsteps came closer, stopped.

Now I couldn't lock it, the noise of the key would draw more attention.

For a moment it seemed they were leaving, but they came back fast, the noise of the door handle woke Cosme and there in the room was the killer.

Cosme pulled the sheet up to his chest. I'd never noticed how big he was, Paulina's husband. He must have been almost six feet six, that ox stare, my jaw must have dropped open. He saw straightaway that we were naked. And smelt the scent of wood with cum and clean sweat. His legs wobbled, they wanted out. His hands made a strange gesture, like they were holding a hat and squeezing the brim. It's an old gesture: the peasants would do it for their overlords, the farm foremen for their land barons, the bureaucrats for their bosses. The timidity of the poor in the big house. Except by then almost no one wore a hat anymore.

He apologized without saying sorry, tried to mutter something else and couldn't. His pants were dirty with mud, his shirt with brown patches of sweat, his hair with cement dust, how could they let him into the movie theater like that? He turned and went to leave. He'd surely come looking for Paulina, no doubt my dad had let him in, everything has a simple explanation. But before he turned away, Cosme propped himself up on one arm, a real little man, and asked what he was doing there.

That was the moment my friend's death began.

Nothing, muttered the killer, then stamped his foot like a horse to snort his hatred and left. My Cosme would only see him again at the hour of his death. I never would.

66

ME: Come here, give me a hug.

On TV, a cartoon. A skinny boy and a stocky, chubby kid building a tree house, hammering in slow motion, a booming orchestra in the background (a variation of Prokofiev's "Dance of the Knights" with bass drums). The chubby kid wobbles, he's going to fall. The boy comes to give me a hug, but always with half an eye fixed on the TV, an expression of relaxed obligation. The hug of a son without fear, loved every day. (No, it's the bendy-skinny one who falls.)

When he clings to me, my neck clicks. I laugh at the wide-eyed look on his face. I don't break that easily. (*Pause*) How he looks like his grandfather.

The killer's face I haven't forgotten. Twenty-six stab wounds to the thorax, I wonder if the police noticed the smell of cinnamon hidden amid the stench of dried blood. My Cosme was found at five o'clock on a Monday afternoon, by a woman I imagine as having a big butt and dressed all in yellow, with two black dogs on leashes. The dogs caught the scent and followed it. He was face down, in just his underpants, in the high grass of the old slave house (where else would the killer think to dump the body?). His T-shirt was in the middle of the street, two blocks away. His pants next to the corpse. Skin bronzed by the afternoon sun, shoulders scorched red. If he'd been alive, he wouldn't have been able to sleep that night. His face without a single scratch, just dirtied a little with soil.

The killer went to get him at the school gates. My Cosme went with him (because?), because they were going the same way, because he was like those poor girls who, even with honor and self-respect to spare, give themselves up too easily. I don't know what they said to each other. Just after midday. ∴∵ When they were out of sight of his teachers and classmates, he grabbed him by the head, with one hand, and started dragging.

The ground crackles in Queím. Cosme must have shouted, but no one came to the rescue. Because? Because it was no one's business, no doubt the boy was impossible, everyone knows they're impossible, these boys. He struggled, managed to break free, tried to run, but he was useless at PE. A tangle of feet, slap, slap, the killer much more predatory than Cosme, who had only ever chased after my sister and never caught her. At some point, the killer grabbed him by his foot, he must already have been unconscious (because?). That was how he lost his T-shirt (because?).

Time of death: approximately 1:00 p.m. ⸭⸮

The murder weapon disappeared. The killer fled. May the worms that tenderly lick your bones never give you rest, Adriano of surname unknown, great-grandson of all the stenches and great-grandfather of the everlasting effluents. Pustule of smallpox on the face of the Aztec emperor! May souls exist and may yours drink only sour milk, devil of the world, candidiasis of the world! Killer! Imagine God's tiredness on the eighth day, right after inventing this race of seed spillers, this race of conquistadors and record breakers, of Himalayan mountaineers, men and women who build the biggest houses of cards, pull trucks with their ears, construct the tallest buildings and start the biggest snowball fights in history and then they die. Then they die, the morons! And they spent their whole lives stuck in traffic, complaining of sleepiness and hunger and of not being loved. Every now and then they have sex with a stranger they met on the bus and sleep snuggled together at the motel, because they're always so sleepy. And they wake up thinking that all life's exclamations are fizzing in their blood, and it's time to photocopy their flesh onto other flesh. The son is born and the father runs off and the mother says this one will be called Adriano, when he could just as well be called José, Luís das Côrtes or Maria Odete. It's the perpetration of the species, the hairy species of those who know they're going to die, but study to finally get that mediocre job at the courthouse and their crooked teeth fixed and their own home and an ungrateful kid and then they die, the morons! The kids will be born with crooked teeth too, the morons. May your soul turn gray and snuff out the sun ⸭⸮ and may the sun snuff out the living for the last time, and torture them too, including me, who can't stand myself, dead pig burning in my guts! Heard of Boskop Man? He was a relative of ours who lived around ten thousand years ago in Africa. He was more intelligent than us, his brain was bigger, his teeth were smaller. Boskop Man was the man of the future. We killed Boskop Man. *Homo sapiens* killed Boskop Man. Ten thousand years ago, we killed the man of the future. Because? Because we did! May the planet be left to other races, other races require no solace. We're exhausted. Only a tired species invents the armored car, telemarketing and nose jobs. And it's too late to die gracefully. May the king vulture assume the throne of the president of this republic and take us all to the grave. The congressmen and their brothers-in-law and the lawyers and the doctors and the police and the thieves. And the miracle workers of Cinelândia and of the temples. And the writers who insist on writing books for adults who shit themselves over having their income tax audited. And those who are tax-exempt. And the chocoholics. And the cinephiles. And all the great composers of great music and the inventors of the airplane. And those who don't sully their hands with money. And the old women who look like wax figures. And the skinny girls who drink coffee with sweetener. And the dead slaves, what would they say if they knew today's diets condemn the sugar they grew? And the museum workers, who insist on remembering. And the secondhand-store owners, and the secondhand-store customers. And everyone who looks back fondly. And everyone who thinks it matters. And the gravediggers. Our destiny is to be geology and there's nobody left in the world who knows what geology is. Adriano, this is the last revelation before oblivion. There's my neighbor listening to the same Nelson Cavaquinho record: "The sun ... shall shine once again. The light ... shall reach our hearts ..." It's beautiful. ⁂ It was my mother who gave me the news. Dad didn't have the courage. I was sleeping, the sleep of a teenager who knows things come to an end, but doesn't truly know. She came in and said wake up, your friend is dead. And put her hand on my shoulder. She didn't hug me. Mama hugged me many times after that, but she didn't think to do it then. She explained what had happened, such a thing you only read about in the newspaper, child killers, a maniac in Queím. The whole gang saw the corpse, but there was no way I'd be going, I wouldn't be setting foot outside the house again, that's what she said. I know she was hoping to see the composite sketch of the killer in the newspapers, but they didn't play ball. After that day, she wouldn't let me out of her sight, I stopped playing in the street, I never saw Tiziu again. Later Dad hugged me, because the ground had opened up beneath him. He hugged me hard and I had to hang on to my crutches. He saw the body too, followed the autopsy. He always called the police "the polis," which is weird, because he was an educated man. He hugged Mama too. She let herself be hugged, then went back to her egg room. They never slept together again. Because? Because they didn't. Paulina was in the middle of it, trying to help, she didn't know the father of her baby had fled. She walked around the house in a daze, afraid to intrude where she shouldn't. A few of my dad's friends showed up too, they were fat, all of them, with thick eyebrows. Dress shirts. Humans invented the shirts and the shoes that cause calluses to later invent the belts and the creams and the foot powders. Because? Because they did! The same race that made chimneys and now recycles plastic bottles. It makes no difference. This planet that began in mud will end in mud: everyone likes a little symmetry. It's bigger than us. Grumá is stuck on "Last Judgment," the song finishes and he puts it back on: "The seed ... of evil will be burnt." And I grew up sadder than a pigeon. As an adult I became angry, useless and grubby. My dad always said a pigeon is a rat with wings, because it's full of diseases. I don't have wings. I'm what nobody wants to think about when they're having lunch. This heat, this sweat that never springs properly from my pores! ∴ ̖ The murder ruled the rest of my life. I was colonized by it. Only rarely am I able to see beauty in things: at the barbershop, for example, I think it's beautiful how everyone gets their hair cut without thinking about how long it took for the hairs to grow and how they keep on growing after death, at least for a while. Or is it the flesh that wrinkles. I find some men beautiful and feel desire, but I find all children sad, for example. I don't see the charm in poetry, in tap dancing, in the singer Chico Buarque or in watching thrillers. I get sick when I smell cinnamon, I actually throw up. I once got into a taxi that had some of those air-freshener sachets hanging from the rearview mirror. The car didn't have air-conditioning, the rear windows wouldn't open. The taxi driver told me about all the people who had wronged him, he kept a list in the glove compartment: one who betrayed him, another who didn't return something he'd borrowed, a friend who'd stopped calling him … the minor grievances of a man terrified of smelling bad. When I noticed that between the sachets of strawberry and eucalyptus there was one of cinnamon, I puked on his arm and thighs. He still took me to the hospital, almost half an hour away (I was going for some tests on my good leg, varicose veins). Him a terrible mess, stinking and not saying a word, and me still nauseous, but now with an empty stomach. The smell of the sachets, of heat, of vomit, of our deodorants. I apologized over and over, he just replied: uh-huh. I tried to pay the fare (R$43.20, which I rounded up to R$45), but he refused. I must have joined that list of villains, another scumbag among the scumbags—and a scumbag's money he wouldn't take. Who cares, killer? What's important is that our wages last the month. What's important is knowing who's screwing whom in the office, in the palace of government and in the soap operas. And what about this inflation? My Cosme was raped before and after he died. They found out at the autopsy. The killer was considerate enough to put the underpants back on the corpse. It was Mama who told me, but only much later, like someone who tells you they once went to Maceió or Paraty and it was pretty good, but they ate a stuffed crab shell that didn't agree with them. We were drinking coffee, with carrot cake and butter biscuits, the kind that come in tins with Swiss scenery on them. Abused, brutalized, assfucked, violated, raped, buggered, torn open, undone, broken in two. If you must know, it was he who fucked me. Every time. With almond oil stolen from my ma, ma, mama. Isn't that what bothers you? So, I'm the one who should be dead, stabbed to death at noon. ⋮ And no one knew where the killer fled to. I don't know if the police went after him, probably not. The biggest danger for a boy is touching an exposed wire and bye-bye, that's what I thought when I was a kid. I don't know if this truth commission they have nowadays knew my father was in the basements giving the tortured their medicine. I stay away from the news. I avoid it, never read it. I change the channel. Did the victims ask themselves if that doctor in the basement had children? If they'd known about me, would they have considered me the heir to his cowardice? Who knows, the victims of these types of things are always semi-saintlike, full of benevolence. Even their way of speaking changes. The way they move their hands, like a person offering food to someone with no money. I changed, but in a different way. I don't think they'd blame me, they wouldn't hate me for what I inherited, but one thing's for sure: my father is in my blood. Perhaps Emílio Médici, the dictator president with the emaciated bulldog face, is in there too. Who knows. Killer, your grandson is the spitting image of you. You ran off before his mother was born, and his father ran off before the kid was born. Your father ran off too, but the women remained, as they almost always do, so motherlike. They're so good! From mother to mother, he's ended up here at home with me. He just gave me a hug. Isn't that convenient? Now the exposed wire is me. There he is, the boy, with his back to me. On TV, chubby and skinny have built the tree house, it's just missing a roof. Now they're sawing a window in the wall with one of those two-man saws. The chubby one is inside the little house and the skinny one is outside the little house, their blindness causing great confusion. All I have to do is go into the kitchen, pull a bread knife out of the drawer, and stick it in the back of his neck. I'll put on the Nelson Cavaquinho CD, to muffle the screams. The boy won't complain, he'll just turn up the volume on the TV, like he always does when I make noise. Over at Grumá's place, the music has started again, the same song. The beginning of the record is a *tradedala-daladalada-lada-lao* played on cavaquinho and guitar. (*Pause*) "The sun ... shall shine once again." ♪, ♪ There'll come a moment when the "Last Judgment" in here will seem like an echo of my neighbor's "Last Judgment," the two will almost coincide: "The light (*the light ...*) ... shall reach (*shall reach ...*) ... our hearts (*our hearts ...*)." I don't know if I'll have the energy to go all the way, I don't know whether to try to hit the boy's jugular or try to strangle him (with my hands? A belt?), whether I'll have the strength to bury the knife in the pit of his collarbone. A lot of blood will be spilled. ♪, ♪ I didn't have time to buy lead pellets—it would have been more practical: just put them in his food and wait. I could go into the kitchen to look for rat poison, but I've never bought rat poison in my life. Funnily enough, there are almost no rats in Queím; plenty of pigeons, plenty of cockroaches. A knife it'll have to be. The bread knife in the apartment is a foot long, the blade is all wavy, stainless steel, the handle fake ivory. It's very light (for its size, it should be heavier), I'll drop it as soon as I take it out of the drawer. A clumsy juggling move—oops, oops, oh—and the knife will fly away, almost ending up under the fridge. When I lean on the fridge door to bend down and get it, everything will slide away from me and I'll fall on my backside. Adrenaline will begin to press on my chest, heart, heat, sweat. At last, sweat. I'll spend a few moments panting, staring at the knife on the floor. My trembling fingers will reach for it, it'll slip away. Trembling with anticipation, not cowardice. I'll get up with less difficulty than usual, almost without needing my cane—it's the impulse of the blood. My fist tight around the handle. I'll go. I'll go and there will be the kid, his back bare, brown. He didn't go to school today. On TV, the lunchtime news, the traffic bulletin, news of the police operation to retake control of the favelas. The hairs on the back of his neck will stand up though he won't know why. He'll hear the tap-tap of the cane, but won't turn around. Even if I called his name twice he wouldn't turn around, only on the third. The *cavaquinho*, the guitar, the *lada-lao*. (*Pause*) Go, Nelson! "The sun … shall shine … once (*The sun …*) again …" My left hand grips his left shoulder—for a few seconds he thinks it's a joke, he makes like he's going to hawhawha—and my right hand sticks the bread knife under his right shoulder. My cane falls to the floor.

("Shall shine … once again …")

I hold myself up with the knife, firmly buried in the boy's ribs. It didn't hit a single bone, went straight into the soft organs. I take a deep breath. Some blood, not much, blooms around the embedded blade. "I want to have eyes … (*have eyes …*) to see …" The boy didn't scream. (*to see … the evil disappear …*) Waves of adrenaline. That revelation experienced by those who kill for the first time. I don't see his dead man's grimace. The world has only one frontier: on this side, all of us who have killed someone.

("The evil disappear …")

The chorus of women's voices comes in. "Love … will be eternal once again …" (× 3) and it's over. Dead. At my neighbor's house, "Last Judgment" starts again, Grumá is hooked on this song. Here, the record plays on as if nothing has happened: "When I step on dry leaves / Fallen from a mango tree …" On TV, a commercial for washing powder. Can't take the knife out, or blood will spill all over the place, a creamy cascade down the boy's back and chest will flood the floor, it'll be hell to clean it later. I have to be careful when I reach down to get my cane, so I don't pull the blade downward and rip his back in half. His delicate skin will open like a raw sausage, his guts spewed out whole, two hunks of flesh on either side, one forty, the other sixty or so pounds. Each chunk of viscera will hit the floor and split in two, and those two will split into eight, and so on, until I'd never be able to get the place clean again. The body has approximately twenty-six feet of gut, Brazil has five thousand miles of coastline, my living room is thirty-six square feet. Every inch of the wooden floor would be filthy with entrails. I'd have no dry floor on which to rest my cane, I'd slip, I'd even be in danger of breaking my femur, my pelvis or worse, God forbid. And then there'd be the smell of intestine. I'd have to pick everything up and put it in a plastic bag, then wash and disinfect, wash and wash and disinfect and burn the used rags. I probably haven't got any black bags; I only buy the blue ones. Or I use the ones from the supermarket, which are white, almost see-through. But I wouldn't have the strength to carry the whole small corpse outside either. I don't have a car, I couldn't call a taxi. Where would I dispose of the body? At the old slave house? Today it's a parking lot. I'd drop the kid right there, between two cars, this year's models, his left leg pressed against the door of a blowfly-green Fiat Palio 99. In the middle of the night. A cripple dragging his leg and dragging a corpse by the leg. I'd have to get in the lift, go past the doorman, past the tree the building manager wants to have cut down. And from here to there it's a good few blocks. I'd have to live with the corpse until nightfall, a little hunk of meat propped up in front of the TV, a pearly plastic handle stuck in its shoulder. After a few hours, I'd get used to its presence, and the knife would start to look like one of those toys you put on your head, a plastic arch with a knife handle on one side and the bloody blade on the other. So, in the position the boy always sat, and with the TV on, it would look like he's almost alive. Maybe I'd even catch myself talking to him.

ME: Are you hungry? Want some lunch?

ME: Do you want to watch a documentary?

ME: Have you had a shower today?

ME: Are you going to school tomorrow?

ME: Are you hungry? Want some dinner?

How long does it take for the dead to start to stink?

65

RENATO: What's up?

On TV, chubby and skinny are, at last, building the tree house roof. The boy looks at me. It's been a while since he's looked at me that way, for so long and without turning back to see what's happening on the screen. I ask for another hug. He gives me one. I ask if he's hungry. He isn't. Is he going to school tomorrow?

RENATO: Tomorrow's Sunday.

The chubby one falls from the tree. He makes a hole in the ground in the garden, and keeps on falling, piercing a hole through the middle of the planet and falling until he falls into the sky, wheee, then falls back down to earth again, whooo, landing on his backside.

He's landed in China.

And he doesn't know how to speak Chinese.

64

I once knocked over a dog. It was a street dog, which had been sitting next to me on the pavement for a long time, as though I were its owner. Dogs get attached easily. I didn't give it food, I didn't tickle its ears or anything. It stayed by my side, on guard. It must have thought I was a beggar.

I stuck my crutch behind its front paws and yanked. For no reason. Out of boredom, I think. It took a step and fell flat on its face, whined, but soon got up and looked right at me, like Renato did. Nobody was with me, but I felt terrible shame, I regretted it straightaway. I hugged the dog. It didn't understand and ran away from me. (So much misplaced tenderness in this life.)

ME: You'll never forget me, will you?

He shakes his head. Smiles. Puts his finger to his forehead.

RENATO: I'm good at remembering.

63

The day after, I woke and my Cosme's desire was no longer in the world. His body was out there, rotting on a table at the mortuary, moved only by the coroner's hands, examining, certifying, trying to slow the decay. The smell of formaldehyde. From the window I could see a white sky that wasn't even close to promising rain, just this cloudy monotony, sweat on something dirty. It was hatred floating free, completely filling the air. Hate is an appendage of the world. Something within the reach of anyone who wants to grab it, let it fester and do whatever they want with it.

(The belly of my eye was throbbing. I was tired. I haven't slept well ever since.)

My sister was sitting on the edge of the bed, head lowered, waiting for me to wake up. She was looking at her nails the way girls do: with the hands open, palms facing downward, because looking at your nails with hands half-closed, wrists facing upward, was a boy thing. She said good morning, her swollen face still a little weepy. Then she made that grin of hers, the grin of somebody who wants to tell/hear secrets. It was strange: she grinned, but the rest of her face remained sad, only her mouth changed. And, over her sad face, there was still the revolted expression she'd acquired after menarche. I only saw that exact grin twice: when my Cosme died and when Mama died.

She wanted to tell me a few things:

1) she knew Cosme had been murdered;
2) she knew what we did, he and I;
3) Mama didn't know, neither did Dad;
4) she wasn't going to tell anyone;
5) she loved me.

62

The funeral was closed-casket, but there was a little glass window to see the face, the face hadn't been stabbed and didn't have scratches. The rest of the body was covered in white flowers. His face was fat and gray, a puffer fish full of water.

At the time, Queím had ≈ 9,000 residents (in the 2010 census, it had exactly 23,567). At least two hundred of those attended the burial. The joyful heart of the people, who come together when tragedy strikes. A people of solidarity, the Brazilian people. I doubt that 3 percent of those who came knew who he was, even fewer that he did what he did with me. The offended old women stayed at home, with their young ladies in tow. The young ladies get old and that's just how it is. Unnatural is what the likes of those boys get up to, and nature itself stops them from prospering, just see how they can't have children. If they could, it would be another story. And the young ladies get old—if they're lucky, with lots of children and grandchildren to love. And along come new young ladies, full of hope for bellyfuls of babies. The joyful heart of the people. In the cemetery, they even sang to God, some cried out for justice, like someone celebrating a goal. They clapped as Dad threw the first handful of lime into the grave. They only didn't make T-shirts with my Cosme's photo because it was the 1970s and there wasn't a single photo of him, nor were there any photographers to record the general commotion.

I couldn't carry the coffin. Naturally, I would have been one of the bearers, and for a few moments Dad forgot I couldn't do it: he even called for me, but then he looked embarrassed and called for someone, anyone else.

I limped after them to the grave.

From the back came a boy, beating the crowd to the foot of the grave, where my dad and I were (Mama and Joana didn't go to the funeral). His name was Caíque, Caio, I don't know. He was from my school, a few years above me. A square-jawed, handsome boy, the color of copper (a typical S.S.K. ♂). The kids in the lower years were afraid of him because he looked mean, because he was older and stronger. I didn't know him and he hadn't known I existed until my Cosme died. But there he was squeezing through, saying excuse me and pushing until he found me. Then he gave me a hug, said something crude and tender and left. He didn't even speak to my father.

61

What happened after my Cosme was dead and buried: nothing. A man ran away the same day, but the police decided his flight had much more to do with the swollen belly of his woman than the stabbed belly of the boy. That was what made real sense. Pure coincidence, that's what they decided. He had nothing to do with the family of his woman's employers, that's what they decided. The investigation starved to death. A random, motiveless crime and therefore it was impossible to find the culprit. That's what they decided. Not one police officer came to talk to me. Dad didn't hire a private detective because nobody actually does that. He believed in the police. Mama believed in the police, my sister believed. The two hundred indigents from the cemetery too: they went back home to work out how, dear God, to scrape together the money for the coming month. That's how it all ended up, only I couldn't leave the house anymore. Today, if you search for Cosme's full name on Google, nothing comes up.

60

A few days later, I went to confront Dad, to ask him what he thought, and to tell him what I was certain of. A delicate situation, because I couldn't tell him everything, but also I couldn't say nothing. It would be a man-to-man conversation, so I got myself ready to go and talk to him: a shirt with a collar, slacks, the same shoes I wore to the funeral. Comb, toothbrush, deodorant.

He was sitting on the double bed, legs crossed and with a plate in front of him. On the plate, a slab of Minas Gerais cheese he was cutting with a meat knife. He was jabbing the blade into each slice and lifting them to his mouth. His feet were swollen, like those of an aged baby, toenails dirty in the corners. When I came in, he asked, amused, why I was all dressed up like that. "Want some cheese?" No. The smell of a sickroom, but of someone with an ordinary sickness: flu, bowel disorders. He'd slept there alone for months.

As I hadn't rehearsed what I was going to say, I said it all in one go: "It was Paulina's husband who killed Cosme."

He burst out laughing. (Because?) All the orifices in his body opened to hawhawha, hawhawhawha. It was as if I'd slipped the perfect joke in at just the right moment: while he was eating cheese, while everything was still sad. A funeral joke. What he least expected. The smell of sickness got worse, it was the breath coming out of all his orifices. A chewed piece of cheese flew onto the sheet. (Because?) All my life I've had the feeling that most people know things I've never even imagined. And the vice versa didn't work so well: what I knew and almost no one else knew, almost no one else would want to know anyway. I was ashamed, but my father was more so. He quickly cut short the laugh, and his rubbery face melted. His toes curled inward. The fingers of his hand were thick and squashed the spat-out cheese onto the sheet when he tried to clean it. He ran his fingernail over it, trying to get it off. It didn't work. It turned into a stain. A white stain on a white sheet.

He discovered then and there that I'd resent him forever.

He relaxed his toes.

He ate another slice of cheese.

I left.

The Paulina question, there was still Paulina, pregnant and dazed in the middle of our house. Once back from the funeral, we found her sitting in the kitchen crying. (Our kitchen had a pale-blue Formica table and chairs. On the table, a bluish glass vase imitating a pineapple husk. Empty.) When she saw me, she opened her arms and tried to speak: her mouth opened and closed, spit stuck to her lips, but no words came out. I hugged her. I was crying too. She soon extended the hug to fit my father, who gave in without any of the inhibitions of a boss. As Dad was standing up, Paulina's face was at the height of his waist.

She wasn't fired, nor did she think about giving notice. She was the victim of the same macho spree, from the same macho, as I was. I was forced to live alongside her. At first I was angry, then I got used to it. They all believed the killer's identity was a mystery. In the end, it may as well have been. Here, no mystery was ever solved, for just that reason.

Today I feel tenderness toward her. Paulina remained in the family until my parents' divorce. In the end, when the ornamental eggs consumed my mother's attention completely, it was Paulina who took on her responsibilities. Despite the lamentable state of his pajamas and his lack of hygiene at weekends, Dad still put food on the table and paid Paulina's salary, which didn't stop her from scolding him—wet towel on the bed, wasted bread (offends Jesus), flip-flops the right way up (or your mother dies), etc. She had a whole book of superstitions. Forbidden: mango with milk; bringing flowers bought at the cemetery gate into the house; putting clothes on inside out (holds one back in life); walking under ladders; breaking mirrors; spilling salt (sign of a family quarrel); dreaming about the TV star Silvio Santos (financial misfortune); pointing at

stars (causes a wart on the tip of the finger); killing an inno-
cent little cricket; cutting off a gecko's tail (problems having a
baby in the future). But we could, for example, eat ants, which
was good for the eyes.

"Ever seen an anteater with glasses?"

58

ME: You won't disappear again, like that other time.

Renatinho hehhehes and says no, no. The other day, I asked
him if he thought Anunciação, the woman who took care of
him, missed him. He gave the same answer: he hehhehed and
said no, no. Nor Carla, who was the girl who lived with them.
He always made sure to explain that she wasn't his sister. He
owed them nothing.

He's stuck with me.

RENATO: What do you call those white streaks that float in
your eye when you close your eyes?

ME: I don't know.

RENATO: Like when you get punched in the eye.

I've never been punched in the eye.

57

Mama wasn't all that sorry. Now, when I reread the bitter letters she left me, I realize she thought Cosme was predestined
to disappear, that, as the child born to one of Dad's victims,
he'd become one of Dad's victims himself. It's one of the laws
of life, my darling son. ♥ If my father hadn't brought him
to Queím, he would still be alive, lost in Barbacena with his
humble destiny (policeman, night watchman, lowly council

bureaucrat). But it was better to go on barely existing than to die for good, wasn't it? That was what she wanted to say.

Dead, Cosme had truly died for her.

Her life went on the same, wine and ornamental eggs (lish polish polishpo lishpo) and liver with onions (her favorite meal). I was the one who wasn't allowed to leave the house again. Every now and then, she would call out my name from inside her room, to see where I was. I was always close by. I never disobeyed my mama.

Renato comes and gives me a kiss on the cheek, mouth slightly open. The sides of my neck, up to my ears, tingle.

A Sun Inside
the House

At first you think it's Saddam Hussein. He used to be on TV a lot, so much that the drug dealers took notice and stapled his face to their little bags of cocaine: a piece of paper with Saddam's face photocopied in black and white, the name of the dealer's corner underneath and the amount of powder. The name of the biggest corner in Queím changed from Salto Azul to Baghdad.

But it isn't Saddam Hussein. He died how long ago? Almost ten years. My God, it seems like yesterday.

In Camilo's living room, it isn't Saddam. It's another dead man, more recent, on TV. But the resemblance is incredible.

The boy Renato, glued to it.

TV: … in the house where political prisoners were tortured and killed …

CAMILO: Change the channel.

The boy doesn't hear.

CAMILO: Renato!

TV: … Colonel Paulo Malhães, "Doctor Pablo," broke his silence …

RENATO: Paulo Malhães was found dead in April 2014 …

TV: … at his house in Nova Iguaçu, in Baixada Fluminense …

GRUMÁ: How many times has the kid seen this?

CAMILO: He has a good memory.

GRUMÁ: He must be a good student.

Grumá goes into the kitchen to check the pig, which is already making the whole house smell of lemon. This time it was his fridge that had given out. And a pork chop without cold beer is no good. Better to do it at Camilo's place. Camilo had offered his credit card to buy a new one, but his friend refused.

And it was Grumá who bought this pig. It wasn't an accidental pig, no. In fact, his sister didn't even breed pigs on the Nova Iguaçu farm anymore. He knocked on the door with almost the entire animal, chopped up and packed in white plastic bags with the red logo of the União Butchers. The head hadn't come with it.

Discounting the head, how much had the pig cost? More than the R$48.96 that Grumá made from the purchase of the oven.

55

Grumá has seen the boy around the neighborhood. He knows he isn't Camilo's son, but who knows whose he is. Is he going to bring him up?

CAMILO: I'm giving him some books to read.

That's good. Sitting in front of the TV all the time melts the eyes. Nobody wants to buy glasses for a ten-year-old kid with bad eyes.

Camilo has given the boy *Journey to the Center of the Earth* and bought some magazines on motherhood, those modern ones, to read, because nowadays you can't beat them, because who knows how to bring up a child: nobody.

GRUMÁ: Not even a quick slippering?

Grumá says he took a few good beatings, and laughs. Clog and belt, with the buckle side! not the soft tail. Tiziu's mother whipped him with a quince branch, leaving painful little snakes on his black legs and back. Iguatemi's father preferred the smack on the backside or on the fugitive legs. Can you spank? "Under certain circumstances, a little slap ..." is what the magazines say. "Physical marks, such as redness and bruises, are a sign that the parents have gone too far," but every mother is sovereign and knows what she's doing, is what the magazines say. Camilo isn't going to beat him, it's decided. He was never beaten by his parents. He wouldn't even have the strength to confront Renato. He's growing. He only had to kick Camilo's cane away once, and the respect would be gone.

54

Grumá reappeared like it was nothing, without apologizing or asking forgiveness for the months of absence. He rang the doorbell and came in, a bottle of (local) whisky in his hand. He'd won on the *bicho*, a ram ticket: 7126, right on the head, that's what he said. He smiled. If he hadn't won on the *bicho*, he'd still be smiling.

The night before, he'd dreamed he'd enrolled in a school for butlers. He wasn't young, he was already an old mule. He put on a suit and tie and went to learn to be a butler, like the ones in films. In the dream the school was inside a church in Glória, and the teacher taught them how to stick their noses in the air and hold trays, but in the end the pupils became priests, not butlers. That's how they trick you.

When he woke up, he consulted his *Book of Dreams* and was left in doubt: had he dreamed of a church (a cat ticket: 9356), a priest (snake: 0234) or a butler (ram: 7126)? He couldn't remember if he became a priest or a butler in the dream, but what he really wanted to be was a butler, so he put all the money he had on the ram, right on the head: ticket seven one two six.

GRUMÁ: What did you dream about last night?

CAMILO: I don't remember.

GRUMÁ: Let's arrange a date and you dream and tell me about it.

They arranged it.

GRUMÁ: I'll bring the pig.

CAMILO: You know that pork makes me sick?

(*Laughter, first from one, then both*)

GRUMÁ: Keep the whisky. I'll bring another bottle.

53

Eleven at night, the pig eaten, Renato sleeping, Camilo's intestines still at ease. They open the new bottle of whisky and get the *Book of Dreams* from Gruma's place. Put more beer in the fridge?

GRUMÁ: What did you dream about last night?

CAMILO: It's too late to play now.

GRUMÁ: You'll have to have another dream. I dream every day. Today it was about an egg. Egg on top of a steak.

Dreaming about eggs, according to the book, means pregnancy in the family, but everything will turn out well. You have to play the rooster, 0449. Dream about bones? Problems at work, the end of a sexual relationship: pig, 2469. Dream about a school report card? Put it on the camel. About TV? Play on the dog and prepare yourself for long business trips. About steak? Play the cow. Eating steak in a dream means you should trust your intuition more.

More whisky and the emotions grow. They look up what

it means to dream about the sea, which for Grumá is a truly beautiful thing. Dream of a calm sea: welcome news from afar. A stormy sea: problems in the future. But the animal is the same for both: the horse. Camilo hasn't seen the sea for a long time.

GRUMÁ: I'm going to take a piss.

On the way back, more whisky and beer and they skip to the entry for "friend." "Friend" or "Dead friend"?

They exchange vows. They really like each other, etc., they really fuckin' do. The close bonds of men with loose bladders. More beer. They promise that tomorrow they'll both play on the friend. Never on the dead friend.

> To dream about a friend is a wonderful thing.
> Dreaming about a friend symbolizes sincere friendships, always being ready to help, always taking an interest.
> Dreaming about a friend also means someone on the outside will bring you long-awaited good news.
>
> ANIMAL = Alligator | LUCKY NUMBERS: 1359

And to dream about love at first sight? That's the peacock! And forbidden love? Mmm, the cobra. And a free sample? Rabbit!

And what is it if I dream about my mother? Grumá really misses his mother.

52

At confession time, the bottle practically empty, Grumá sobs an enormous story about when he had a truck and a woman in Saquarema. A big blue Mercedes, '85, strong as an ox. He had to sell it after a run-in with the highway patrol.

In return, Camilo tries to show his friend his notebooks. School notebooks, ten subjects, spiral-bound with photos of surfers and race cars on the covers. His whole life is in them. His handwriting is good. Maybe he's the only one who's read them, he wants to burn it all before he dies, so that his son doesn't know anything.

But it's a lot to take in. Grumá isn't much of a reader, no. He'd take five years. He'd rather hear it from his mouth.

They go into the kitchen, better, if the boy wakes up they'll hear him.

51

He tells him about his journalist sister, who Grumá doesn't know because she isn't on the TV news. About his mother, who collected ornamental eggs—if he'd kept them, they could have been resold, collector's items. About the maids. About his dad the doctor.

He tells him that his mother once went to the laundry room and tipped a cup of black coffee onto her husband's clothes, which were soaking in a bucket. His friend laughs. He's seen them do worse.

And he talks about his Cosme, in details that his triple-plastered friend knows to listen to with that sailor's face of his: wind on his cheeks, eyes squinting at the horizon. One man with another man, two young boys, Grumá isn't sure about that, no. Though of course, he's never seen Camilo with a woman. Though not with a man either. Though, already triple-drunk, he remembers that soap opera, what was it? The villain was one of those ... he liked men. He was a villain, but he later became a good guy. Camilo smiles.

(*Pause*)

GRUMÁ: There was one called Sandrinho! In *The Next Victim*!

50

And the documents? The boy's documents. It can't be that easy, where are his certificates? Camilo doesn't know, but he'll go to the clinic. To disappear is easy, to appear is a lot more complicated. And, deep down, as they listen to the carcass of the pig sizzling in the oven, Grumá doesn't entirely believe what he's heard. He always chars the remains of the animal before throwing them away.

CAMILO: Do you know who your father is?

GRUMÁ: No.

CAMILO: Do you have kids?

GRUMÁ: Not that I know of. (*Chuckle*)

CAMILO: Do you know they're going to cut down the tree at the front? Day after tomorrow.

GRUMÁ: About time. I chipped in. You know the old woman from 701 almost broke her elbow? She tripped over the root.

CAMILO: It's not the tree's fault.

GRUMÁ: And what about when you get old?

A burning begins in Camilo's kidneys and bubbles up through his belly, almost to the height of his heart. The whisky helps ignite a stomach bloated with ice-cold beer. The pork liquefies and descends through the intestines, catching fire, pushed by the fumes from the inferno above.

On the banks of the sphincter, lava.

CAMILO: I need to go to the bathroom.

GRUMÁ: Who'll be the boy's godfather?

The first thing that Camilo teaches his son is to eat with his mouth closed and swallow his food before drinking Coca-Cola. Do you want a dog? Renato doesn't, he's had plenty of dogs on the street. Have you been baptized? As he doesn't remember, he says no. Uncle Grumá will be your unofficial godfather. OK.

They won't need to go to church.

The boy's memory is a remarkable thing. He seems to record everything that catches his eye, forgets little—or has learned to forget what suits him: his homework and the dirty plate in the sink. He's a terrible student, he still can't read well. *Journey to the Center of the Earth* has been abandoned in his room for months. Camilo thinks about buying him a computer, he'll need it to do research online. Ten installments of R$71.55 from the big store in the shopping mall. He tells the boy this and doesn't let him forget it. Ten installments of R$71.55.

The kid is smart, he tells Grumá. He's learned to call him "Dad" when he talks about the computer. He can describe an entire film, with the details we forget straightaway, all the colors of the girl's dresses in the order they appear, the name of the policeman's German shepherd. Yesterday he repeated an entire speech he saw on government TV about that petroleum affair. It isn't an ordinary thing. He can't have been to the paediatrician more than twice, imagine if someone took him to a head doctor. That type of ability always comes with a catch, high blood pressure, a stroke, blindness, strange urges.

CAMILO: What do you remember about your dad?

GRUMÁ: Hard to say, out of the blue like that.
CAMILO: He's going to remember everything.
GRUMÁ: I took a lot of beatings.

47

At the boy's first serious flu, Camilo panics. According to the modern mother magazines, "first-time dads overreact when their little pup gets sick," but this is different. He starts coughing like a dog, then develops shortness of breath, whistling in his lungs, an itchiness in the middle of his chest that won't stop. Suddenly, Renato becomes totally phlegmy, his breath sluggish, he can't sleep. Weeks, it lasts. The boy learns to spit beige jelly from his lungs, memorizes the map of the apartment's drains.

CAMILO: How many times have you been to the doctor?
RENATO: Three.

He takes the boy to all the clinics he can, all on the public health service, he can't afford health insurance. The boy has no documents at all and Camilo doesn't have the courage to go and ask the woman who used to look after him. Who knows if she has them. To the bureaucrats at the hospital, he gives the excuse that he's still trying to get copies, they lost everything in a fire, in a house move, in the last flood. Isn't there an authorization that he can sign? There always is.

Doctors, redoctors, rescheduled appointments. Renato likes to take the bus. Viruses, worm medicine, cough syrup. The neurologist at Bonsucesso General Hospital says he's a normal boy, there are people who really do have good memories. Are you the father? Tell his mother everything is fine.

They just want you out of their office. One less problem before lunch. The little one only has catarrh.

The day he met Iguatemi and they went for a beer, he'd told him Knots was a nurse at the Bonsucesso General Hospital, but that had been many years ago. Each time they go there, Camilo asks after Norberto, about a skinny nurse, about Knots? Nobody can tell him anything. There's no one here with that name, they know, because there are almost no male nurses, we're sure of that.

Also, what is he going to say to him?

This is my son?

They're in an emergency department in Queím. A Sunday. Renato coughing, scratching his chest. He scratches so much that he's made a wound, as if his heart had been operated on. He's gotten so used to his runny nose, he doesn't even sniff anymore. There's a crust of mucus under the nostrils, retouched with each brush with his arm. His forearm has a streak of hard snot stuck in the hair, which the kid seems proud of.

A few sick people: the only one Camilo recognizes is Tatuí, who works in his father's carpentry shop. He's broken his arm playing soccer. He's alone, still in his neon-green professional soccer cleats and his shirt from the match: red with a white diagonal stripe, Q.R.C.—Queím Regatta Club. There are no clubs in Queím, much less regatta clubs. The name's just for show. The left elbow swollen purple, elephantiasic. Now that his body has cooled down, Tatuí groans a deep groan. Now who'll help his father in the carpentry shop? The smell of dry sweat reminds Camilo of the day Otávio was hit on the chin, the day he learned how to make himself cum.

He tries to contain an erection.

There are other patients, about ten. The blue-and-white walls of the health center, clean as an advertisement for the Rio de Janeiro state government. The air thin, decontaminated and fresh. The faces a little solemn, but none desperate.

Camilo looks at the toes of a black baby, the pale-black fingers of the hands of the baby's mother, the woman's worried face. The baby sniffles and snuffles and moans, looks like he's going to cry. His little fingers are swollen, his feet two bunches of grapes, full of allergic seeds. Camilo smiles at the mother, waves hello, thinks that everything will be fine, your son will survive, he has to survive, I hope he will.

The baby starts to cry. The other patients don't seem to hear, but Camilo's nerve endings are fireworks, all the exclamations of life bursting through his crippled body. The strange love for someone else's child, who cries, but is not in danger. Nobody there is going to die now. The mother makes a sh-sh-sh, rocks the child, looks embarrassed. Camilo points to his boy.

CAMILO: He has the flu.

The woman smiles, not wanting to talk. He smiles back, while the quiet faces of the other patients sense, in the distance, the haw-haw of death.

44

The boy gets better, of course he does. Other than the four civilizations of worms flourishing in his gut, nothing too serious. Amazing how he never complained about the pain, the doctor says. He must have been in constant pain. His life will be different without this discomfort. (Maybe *now* he thinks something is wrong.) And he's lucky: not one parasite infected his brain. You have to take him to the doctor regularly. He has to: wash his hands, not play in the dirt, avoid undercooked pork, in fact any pork. Just to be safe. Avoid contact with stray animals. Wash the salad and fruit he eats well. The basics. Are you a widower?

Yes.

43

Camilo has never celebrated Carnival. The Queím of his childhood caught fire, those were the only days when the beige dust turned golden-yellow. But he never saw it. His mother wouldn't let him—the *bate-bola* clowns, the ball-beaters, were crueler back then. Some already grown men, in colorful costumes and demon masks, sometimes in gangs, dragging ox bladders attached to strings, which they beat hard on the ground. The smell of raw meat, the dead battered tissue, always spraying what little blood was left of the animal. :,: The blood never drained completely. Nowadays, they use plastic balls, but in those days it was terrifying: they'd scare the boys, knock them down, strip them naked, take the chance to do bad things. Camilo grew up terrified of Carnival.

When he had the antique shop, he opened from Friday to Ash Wednesday, to see the Copacabana revelers, the teenagers, the half-lost recent divorcees, the aging bachelors. Couples brought together by chance would hide in the shopping arcade, the occasional drunk would sit on the benches in the corridor, an unsuspecting passerby who needed a bit of a breather. A Colombina, a Captain America, a hairy baby, a Frida Kahlo, a Super Mario, a nurse.

Sometimes they came into the store. The untidiness inside, the shadows, the singular items, some anecdotal, the cripple behind the counter, everything gave the impression of another

Carnival, deeper, quieter. They looked at the photo albums of the eternally unknown, the hats of people who were probably dead, the radios that no longer worked—they looked at everything with serious faces, even the triple- and quadruple-plastered, even the men dressed as mermaids, with that awkward gait of a costume that hasn't gone right. They left in silence. At most, a smiling wave.

They never bought anything.

Renato has always gone to Carnival, ever since he was little, running free among the glitter, his semibare feet lifting off the ground, a mini *exu* elbowing space among the *blocos*, understanding almost nothing. He always stood up to the *bate-bolas*, with iron bars and rocks, if necessary. Maria Aína used to say that, during Carnival, the entities can't descend to earth, but some break through the barrier. *Erês*, *exus* and other rebellious spirits come to have fun on top of the floats and dance among the people.

When February comes, something in Renato's blood will stir. Camilo can predict it. He'll break three glasses at home, accidentally on purpose, get into more fights at school. If he doesn't let the kid go out, he'll threaten to go back to where he lived before, with his ex-mother. The new clothes, the room with R$9.99 toys, the mornings combed with hair gel and pay-attentions at school, kiss, will be in danger. The new family chains will begin to burn on his wrists.

It's still early December, but the *bloco* drummers are already rehearsing in the streets. The boy wants to go, without knowing where. The becauses that no one knows. Camilo tries to negotiate Carnival. Don't you want a dog? No, I've already had plenty of dogs on the street. Carnival is dangerous. And the boy laughs. You're not going. Oh yes I am. Are not. Am so. Don't you want a computer?

Deal. A computer for Carnival. They'll watch the parade

on TV until the early hours. They'll order pizza, Coca-Cola. Will Portela or Salgueiro take the prize this year? Did you see Mangueira enter? the boy asks, and laughs.

Ten installments of R$71.55.

42

In Camilo's day, most *blocos* paraded along the seafront. All wore tattered strips of crepe paper over their naked bodies and, at the end, the drum section was the first to enter the water, still in formation, dancing and drumming furiously; soon drowning, row by row, from the bell shakers to the bass drums.

When the last drum went under, everyone stopped singing and threw themselves into the sea. The bodies still within the memory of the drumming, dancing without music. The costumes came apart, leaving a few stains of color on the skin, like old whip marks. The instruments were lost in the waves, returned to the sand, worthless, offerings.

He himself never saw it. The sea is a long way off.

41

But Carnival is also a long way off. There is still Christmas, New Year, the reviews of 2014 on TV, to come. For years he hasn't celebrated any of it. At Christmas, an ordinary dinner, beef liver or chicken gizzards, whichever is cheaper. At most he puts raisins in his rice. Sometimes he buys a panettone. The obligatory telephone call from his sister, which goes on longer each year, because the two of them, to make up for it, pad the conversation with Christmas card sayings. On New Year's Eve, he goes to bed at ten.

This year has to be different. The boy. He invites Grumá for Christmas dinner, but his neighbor has other plans. He's going to spend Christmas with his sister in Nova Iguaçu, but he'll leave a present for his godson. There isn't anyone else to invite.

A proper dinner, at least. On the kitchen table, the turkey, a piece of ham spiked with cloves, rice, *farofa*, a chocolate panettone, fruits, pumpkin compote, *canjiquinha*. A banquet for two. Neither he nor the boy will be able to finish it. After three days eating the leftovers, all of it in the bin.

And with so many people going hungry. He remembers how his mother used to kiss the stale bread before throwing it away, because bread was God's food. But if it was God's food it shouldn't go hard from one day to the next.

They'll wear their best clothes. The parties on the TV soaps will keep them company. The characters celebrate Christmas and New Year too, as though they're in the real calendar, a coincidence that still fascinates the boy. He hasn't got to the point where he totally understands the strings behind the little theatre in the corner.

Camilo doesn't know how the boy used to spend his Christmases, if he got presents from his ex-family, if the house was filled with people. He'll buy a few more toys from the shop, a kite, line and wax, a plastic lorry, a few rubber dinosaurs, but what Renato is really going to like is the computer.

When the soap opera is over, he might go a little quiet, but Camilo won't ask why. In another home, his ex-mother will perhaps wonder where he's ended up, if he's all right. She probably knows he's living with the rich cripple from something-or-other street now. Maybe, at Christmas, an impulse will ferment inside her. Maybe she'll want him back. Maybe she'll talk to a cousin, who's a policeman. Maybe rumors will spread.

What's strange is that the boy has never looked out of the window, not even when planes, helicopters go past. He has never waited for his father at the window because Camilo almost never leaves the house, but, deep down, he knows Renato doesn't wait for him because he isn't really his father.

CAMILO: Do you like me?

RENATO: Yes.

He's never asked how much. Afraid that the boy won't respond the way he's seen the other children do, opening their arms as wide as they can and saying this, this much, no this much, no this much more, no this much more.

Between 2 December and Christmas, there's an entire year. The school holidays already drag, Camilo tries to read *Journey to the Center of the Earth* to the boy, but the TV is much better. Renato sits in all the chairs in the house, tries all the R$3.99 spice powders and coughs laughing. This is cinnamon, this is paprika, this is ground cumin. He goes down to the street without asking permission and comes back with bits of wood, broken tiles, plants torn up by the roots, let's make a forest.

Camilo can't say no. The street doesn't bite. Boys need the street.

When Renato comes back, he lies down on the sofa and remembers, or he's tired, or he saw the woman who looked after him before and misses her. Camilo will never ask.

Where love begins no one remembers. The triggers of hate are all easy: the moment she says you're a piece of shit, the stone that strikes the kosher restaurant, the bomb in the house of an aunt in Rafah, the day after the day you weren't invited. One day Camilo asked if he liked condensed-milk biscuits and the boy laughed. He laughed for twenty seconds and said yes, then laughed for another thirty. Laughed at him. Pointed at his face. Why? What are you laughing at? And he laughed more. That's when the hate could have started, but it didn't. It could have started when the kid yelled that he wasn't his father because he wasn't allowed to go outside at eight o'clock at night. But it didn't start.

And that's how Camilo knows he loves his son.

Hate never starts when it might.

38

On the morning of the 14th, the rain begins. The rattling wakes him up, but Camilo doesn't open his eyes. Every year is alike: a few days before Christmas, the downpour begins and only stops just before New Year. The filthy water, regurgitated by the drains, floods the streets and invades the houses. Later the reporters arrive to ask if we've lost everything. They film our faces in close-up, hoping we'll cry. "How are you feeling, *senhora?*" "What does it feel like?"

Throughout the year, the residents try to prepare themselves for the rain, they erect higher walls or dikes, dig canals. It makes no difference. Not even they have any confidence. In the last days of November, when the wind starts to blow harder in the afternoon, they carry their furniture upstairs and wait.

The water arrives brown, with bits of wood, dead cockroaches, drowned dogs, rats dead or alive, some appearing to run on top of the water. It drags away motorbikes and cars, which strike the walls like battering rams. When a wall gives way, the house collapses and everyone dies. Lucky for Camilo, who lives in an apartment.

With every passing year, things get worse, is what they say. It starts to rain earlier. The water rises ever higher. On Rua do Canela, it reaches two and a half meters. The cars floating. The pet dogs. The loose wires crackling with electricity, a danger. God protect those who live close to the ravines.

If it continues like this, they'll have to raise the buildings even higher. Who has the money these days to build a third floor on their house?

And afterward, before New Year's Eve, we wash off the mud that's left on the walls ... The risk of leptospirosis, did you know it's caused by rat piss? On the walls, on the roof of the houses there's rat piss. That's how we live.

You can smell the stench for the rest of the year.

37

Sometimes the sun comes out, but the water doesn't go down and the sky doesn't clear completely. ∴ The children climb on the roofs of buses almost entirely submerged. They shout, hold their noses and dive into the brown water. The helicopters from the TV film it: first the residents on their roofs, waving white sheets as an SOS. Next, the wiring giving off sparks. Next, the kids swimming in the flood.

The news anchor in the studio asks: where are the parents of these children at a time like this? When they cut back to the studio, the anchor looks into the camera like a saddened mother, even if she isn't a mother, even if it's a man. And next, the Civil Defense says this; the mayor decrees that. Other news.

Camilo doesn't want to be the target of the news anchor's disappointed gaze. In Queím, the flooding is good because it creates antibodies, that's what they say. But not for Renato. He's already forbidden him, he'll forbid him again. The boy will laugh, hawhawha at him again.

For the first time, Camilo catches his son looking out of the window. Down below, the flooded street, a few kids swimming: they dive head first, do belly flops, nuclear bombs. It's raining, but the sun threatens. They're trapped, but there's still enough food for two weeks. How they'll buy the things for Christmas dinner, Camilo doesn't know. In previous years, he always had chicken gizzards in the freezer.

The boy doesn't want to hear *Journey to the Center of the Earth*, isn't hungry, doesn't want to watch TV. Camilo doesn't ask anymore.

The sun comes out while he's still at the windowsill. The light lays a yellow strip on the living room floor, with a long, dark slice from the child's shoulders. He's still a child, even if he has a good memory.

Cosme died with scratches bleeding on his back.

A caress on the back of the boy's neck as he looks out of the window. Camilo asks, to be sure, if he doesn't want to go down for a swim. The laugh is quieter, but still a laugh.

RENATO: I don't know how to swim.

RENATO: Do you have a girlfriend?
CAMILO: No, I don't.
RENATO: Did your girlfriend die?

CAMILO: No.

He told the doctor he was a widower and the boy knows what that means.

They're on the way back from the supermarket, Camilo carrying the leg of pork in the hand free of his cane, and his son four plastic bags with the rest of the dinner. They still need the ham, which Grumá has promised to collect from the butcher, no need to pay, it's on me, Merry Christmas, etc. and so on. He'll make *farofa* too, with banana and bacon.

The streets full of mud. Camilo has waterproof boots, like a butcher's, but he prefers to wear flip-flops, like the boy. He forgot to buy a pair of boots for him. The watery clay gets between the toes, the soles of the feet slip on the rubber, threatening to tear the straps of the flip-flops. Watch out for shards of glass. Once home, he washes him thoroughly, sponging between his toes. The boy makes a face, a nervous twitch in his little toe. Perhaps he's dying, the father, perhaps he, the boy, will become a widower. Maybe he really doesn't know what is meant by the word.

RENATO: Didn't your girlfriend die?

CAMILO: No.

The residents wash the pavements with hoses and mops. They're happy, the flood has subsided before Christmas Eve. They're in flip-flops too.

34

A Christmas with two people is always sad. A birthday. A New Year's Eve. It doesn't matter if the two love each other, or how much. Camilo and Renato don't love each other that much, they haven't had time.

The banquet on the kitchen table, lit by fluorescent lamps,

the white-tiled floor shining clinically. The warm perfume of the meats, the disinfectant from the cleaning. Cooked ham and cloves. Eucalyptus air freshener. The sound of the TV from the living room, the news before the soap opera, a flood who-knows-where, the solidarity of the Brazilian people. Every once in a while, cries of joy in the street. In every house there's an amusing uncle; in every uncle, a joke they can't hear ('Mama, I'm fourteen, can I wear a bra? No, João'). Silent forkfuls. Camilo smiles, the boy smiles.

He's going to get a computer.

The next day, or as soon as their stomachs start to feel heavy, there are two of them left. Not three, not the world. It's sad. See on TV how different countries are getting ready to welcome 2015. The phone is silent. Nobody rings the doorbell.

A bad wine is turning to vinegar in the head of Renato's ex-mother, is what Camilo thinks. Something is turning rotten. A flow of old blood, older each year—soon she won't be able to have children. Anunciação. In rubber flip-flops, nails done for the Christmas just past. She thinks about the boy as she drinks black coffee with yesterday's French toast, the sugar that slept in the fridge on her coffee-burnt tongue. The phone doesn't ring.

Carla is still asleep. The relatives who came, an aunt and a cousin, brought presents for the two children: toy cars, a spinning top and two dolls. But the girl is already almost a young lady, why dolls? It's good to practice. These girls have children early these days. They hide the toys for the absent boy. A little blue plastic sedan and a top made of blonde wood, the string already a little grimy. They don't say anything, they don't ask. They leave. They can be reused. There'll always be boys.

Mama, the girl calls her. Renato never did.

It's not exactly that she misses him. Nor pride. But she's going to want the boy back, is what Camilo thinks. She's free of his weight, but her back still remembers, her arms. Did she put him on her lap? He'll never be able to do that. The limbs get used to the pain. They like it. They fill with lactic acid and the future: they want more weight tomorrow, even more later. Camilo knows, he understands the secrets of muscles, because his have atrophied. Nobody rings the doorbell.

It's what his magazines say: "Boys have a deep connection with their mamas." There are no magazines for a world without mamas. But it's mama who brings them up. Dad who brings them up. "Girls meanwhile usually consider their dad the most incredible man on the planet."

The ex-mother is going to want the boy back. If the phone rings on Christmas Day and she tells him that an officer of the court, that her policeman cousin, that she herself is coming to get him. Renatinho will give himself up. He's still a child, everything is final and impotent. He'll cry, maybe he'll cry, let's hope he cries. But no one knocks on the door. The phone.

The phone is going to ring. But, if it rings, it could be anyone.

Glossary

bandido   criminal usually associated with armed, violent crime or membership of armed gang

bate-bolas   frighteningly garbed Carnival clowns (literally "ball-beaters')

bloco   Carnival street band, often followed by large crowds

cachaça   distilled spirit made from fermented sugarcane juice

canjiquinha   dish made with cornmeal porridge and pork

cavaquinho   small guitar-type musical instrument

cruzeiro   Brazilian unit of currency between 1942 and 1994

dejú   Yoruban term, used here as an expression of affection

erês   playful, childlike spirits in the Afro-Brazilian religion of candomblé

exus   candomblé spirits, sometimes described as devils

farofa   toasted cassava/corn flour, popular Brazilian side dish

filhas de santo   female candomblé medium or priestess-type figure

jogo do bicho   street lottery game with tickets based on animal images. Hugely popular, though officially prohibited by law

Kichute   iconic Brazilian trainer/soccer boot, popular in street soccer

macumba   slang term for various Afro-Brazilian religions

macumbeiro   practitioner of *macumba*

mocotó   sweet jelly made from cow's-feet stew

ossí   shortening of Oxóssi, a candomblé divinity. Used here as a term of affection

pombajira   female candomblé spirit, standing for female sexuality and strength

Acknowledgments

When I started *The Love of Singular Men*, I made a public request for future readers to help write a paragraph of the book. I set up a website where I asked them to tell me the name of their first love and, if they chose, their own name. They only had to fill in a form. The list was transcribed in this novel.

They answered. It's amazing how people respond when you ask them about their love. Many told stories, some didn't even give their names, they just wrote to me about their first loves. I understood they didn't want to appear in the book, they just wanted me to know. People I'd never even met told me really sad or funny, or just normal things.

I've kept these stories to myself. To those who participated, my thanks. I'm less singular because of those names. They are my way back to tenderness. (*Pause*) I don't mean they're an amulet. Let's call them an anchor.

Very few people chose to remain anonymous, and the names of their loved ones are at the top of the list. The other names were sent in the order in which they appear in the paragraph. It turned out like the Carlos Drummond de Andrade poem "Quadrilha," except that no one is left out of the story. Or everyone is.

VICTOR HERINGER, 2016

New Directions Paperbooks—a partial listing

*BILINGUAL EDITION

For a complete listing, request a free catalog from New Directions, 80 8th Avenue, New York, NY 10011 or visit us online at ndbooks.com